SEALED

SEALED

NAOMI BOOTH

TITAN BOOKS

Sealed
Print edition ISBN: 9781789091243
E-book edition ISBN: 9781789091250

Published by Titan Books
A division of Titan Publishing Group Ltd
144 Southwark Street, London SE1 0UP
www.titanbooks.com

First Titan edition: July 2019
10 9 8 7 6 5 4 3 2 1

Printed and bound in the United States of America

For Dulcie and Laura

Thy hands fashioned and made me; and now
thou dost turn about and destroy me.

Remember that thou hast made me of clay;
and wilt thou turn me to dust again?

Didst thou not pour me out like milk
and curdle me like cheese?

Thou didst clothe me with skin and flesh, and
knit me together with bones and sinews.

JOB 10:8-11

WE came out here to begin again. We came out here for the clear air and a fresh start. No one said to us: beware of fresh starts. No one said to us: god knows what will begin.

Pete found the house online. Mountain View. We'd only seen pictures, but it looked so good – a whole house, the kind you can only dream of in the city, with scrubbed wooden floors, a bright, enamel kitchen, a verandah with views across the valley – that we took the risk, put down the deposit sight unseen. The drive out took longer than we thought and, by the time we arrived, the van was already parked-up in the driveway. The sun was going down, though it was still light enough, just, to see. I sat in the passenger seat for a while as Pete helped the removal men. The front of the house was pretty in an implausible way, like a house in a picture-book or a holiday brochure: a white chalet, edged with dark-leafed, tropical plants. Behind the house I could see the outline of the mountains in the distance, greying in the dusk, and, nearer-by, lights glimmering in the valley bottom. We never had asked why the house was suddenly vacant or why the rent was so cheap. It's best not to pry, Pete says, it's best not to worry. It'll be nothing, he says: a redundancy, a divorce, a clean, old-fashioned death.

By the time I get out of the car the blokes have already started carrying our boxes into the house. Pete has turned on the lights inside and I dawdle in front of the porch. The plants look weird: it's been a while since I've seen anything this lush. I touch the leaves to check that they're real and they're waxy and cool like synthetic matter, but they tear through when I push with my nail. The blooms are enormous – frilly and faintly obscene. I can hear my mother's voice in my head, naming them for me: gardenia, hibiscus, Angel Ivy. Their fragrance follows me, sweet and morbid on the cooling evening air.

When I get inside Pete grabs my hand, pulls me into the living-room and points to a large box. 'Here,' he says, 'you can sit on this until we get the chairs out.'

'I've been sitting all day,' I say, 'I want to look around.'

'Not while all this is going on,' he says, 'I don't want anyone to bump our bump.' He leans down and kisses my swollen stomach.

The removal men don't talk as they work. They sweat a lot and get everything into the house as quickly as possible.

They've got another long drive ahead of them, back to the city. I watch them working, letting myself imagine what they'll do tomorrow. Sunday in town. Maybe the younger one will lie-in, meet friends for brunch somewhere by the harbour. Bloody Marys and runny yellow yolks. Maybe he'll go to see a movie in one of the old theatres downtown with dusty velvet seats and mice skittering about in the dark. Maybe he'll sleep all day and then get wrecked on dirty beer in a bar by the market. Some of the things that we used to do. I turn my attention to the other man, the older of the two; he's heavy on his feet, grizzled around his muzzle like an old dog. There's something that draws my attention to his eyes, something at the outer corners. The skin of his eyelids is unusually pronounced, making an exaggerated fold. And the skin crinkles up at the outer edges of his eye sockets. I mean, it *really* crinkles, making deep crags whenever he lifts something heavy and grimaces. I pat my fingertips against the edge of my own eye socket: my skin feels soft and slightly puffy. It's hard to imagine *normal* skin cragging like that, loosening and folding away from the face as much as his. Are his eyes too hooded to be healthy? I want to say something, to ask him if he's had it checked out, but I know Pete will flip if I do. I'm supposed to be leaving all of this behind me. I think about it too much, Pete says, and that's the main problem, he says, because when you think about anything too much your thoughts distort the thing itself. Thinking like I do, worrying all the time, Pete says it's like repeating the same word over and over to try to learn it, until the word becomes just sound: and then the sound becomes a kind of hex, a weird noise that conjures something darkly different.

I stay sitting on the box and I watch my things and Pete's things being re-assembled next to one another: my bed-settee next to his shelves, my mother's old dining table surrounded by the camping chairs Pete's dad gave us. I guess this is what it looks like to try to build a life together: cast-offs and old family favourites forced into uneasy covenants; a mess. And I keep being drawn back to the man's eyes, to their ragged corners.

When everything has been unloaded I can't help myself, I whisper to Pete: 'I think there's something going on with that bloke's eyes. I think there might be something… look at his skin… at the edges?'

Pete looks over at the man. He's wiping his forehead on a blanket that a mirror was just wrapped in. He grins when he notices us staring. 'A'right,' he says, 'just about done. Nice place you've got here.'

'Fucksake, Alice,' Pete hisses at me. 'Fresh start, but?' He strides over to the bloke. 'Cracking job, mate,' he says, shaking the man's hand and then clapping him on the back. 'Safe journey back.'

'Beaut of a place this,' the man says, standing in the doorway, jerking his head backwards to indicate the garden and the mountains beyond, disappeared in the darkness now. 'You're best off out of it. I've nippers, you know, and grandchildren. Three of 'em. You don't want 'em growing up in that, do ya? The smogs, Christ knows what else. How long you got to go?' He looks over at me.

'Four weeks,' I say and I look down at my bump. Its swollenness still seems unreal. I barely showed until six months.

'Yep, best off out of it,' he says.

Pete walks him down the path, waves the van off. When he comes back in, he strides about the place, holding his mobile phone up in the air in the corners of the living-room. 'Nope,' he says, 'bugger all connection. You got anything, babe?'

I've stopped keeping my phone close by. I go to my bag and turn it on. The reception icon appears, and then a red cross. 'Nothing,' I say and turn the phone off again.

'Well, you'll be pleased about that,' he says. 'No radiation.'

'Yeah,' I say.

'And no news for you to fixate on.'

'That's right,' I say.

'And no way for you to post online.'

'Uh huh,' I say.

After we've found my mother's old linen and made up the bed Pete's parents gave us, Pete says we should call it a night. 'We're knackered,' he says, 'let's start on the boxes in the morning.' Our cups are still packed away, so we drink from the kitchen tap, scooping water up in our hands and into our mouths. It tastes different: richer than in the city, a hint of iron. 'Christ,' I say, 'Pete, what if it's not filtered?'

'Of course it's filtered,' he says. 'It's not the dark ages out here. There's a pump, I'm sure they mentioned a pump. I'll check everything in the morning.'

'Can we go out onto the verandah?' I ask. 'I need some air.'

''Course.'

From the back of the house there's a clear view straight across the valley towards the mountains. It's dark now, almost midnight, though the darkness is strangely luminous. I can still pick out the flowers in the garden: the greens of leaves are recast in shades of blues. There are jacaranda and oleander flowers gleaming deeply at the furthest edge of the borders and the jarrah trees rustle where the foliage plunges out of sight, disappearing down the steep valley edge.

'It's so lush out here,' I say. 'Why is everything still so… bright?'

'Stars!' Pete says. He sounds excited and kisses the top of my head. 'Poor bub,' he says. 'You're gonna need to get to know the bush. You've been in the city too long.'

1

WE make our first trip into Lakoomba the next day. We spend most of the morning unpacking, surprising ourselves with our own belongings. My mother's old crockery, Pete's dad's old toolkit, stained towels and worn rugs and frayed tablecloths donated by Pete's extended clan. It's like unpacking a stranger's life. Even my clothes look unfamiliar to me, here. Eventually, we get too hungry to continue. It's so hot; Pete's skin is shiny with sweat. He smells warm and sour, as though he's fermenting. 'Let's get a beer,' he says. I dread to think what I look like – I'm in dungarees and my hair's electrified by something out here, my fringe frizzed-up with static. I glance in the mirror; then I remember where we are and I don't bother with lipstick.

The main street in Lakoomba is deserted. Low, white buildings on both sides, blisteringly bright in the sun, and no bugger out on the pavements. Half-way down the main drag the shop-fronts get more dramatic: raised, square facades in creams and browns, with painted shutters. It looks like the American West, after the gold ran out. There are a few trucks parked-up – faded paint-work, rust around the wheel hubs. One that we pass has corroded right through in places, light-blue paint peeling away, the metal-work lifting in a bright copper rash. It looks like it could have been parked-up here for the last century.

Maybe we've come at the wrong time of day. Maybe the locals know to avoid the mid-afternoon heat and the town will spring into life later. Or maybe they're religious out here and nothing opens on a Sunday. We pass a whole run of closed shops and deserted hotels, and then we approach a bar called O'Malley's and there's a thrum of human noise coming from inside. Pete shades his eyes and peers in through a small window. 'It's bloody heaving!' he says. Pete's practically through the door already. I follow, but it takes a while for my eyes to adjust, so I falter at the threshold. I blink a couple of times and see that Pete's already made it to the bar ahead of me. There are lots of men clustered around small circular tables. The place is cramped. I see a bloke nudge another and point in my direction. His mate laughs and then widens his eyes, staring at my belly. He sloshes his beer around and licks his parched lips.

'C'mon, darl,' Pete calls to me from the bar. Darl? He's never called me that before.

'I'll have a pint of your best grog, mate,' Pete says to the barman. 'And a schooner for the lady.'

'I don't want a schooner,' I say, quietly. 'Get me a protected lemonade.'

'Don't be a poof,' he says, loudly. And then more gently, 'Only joking. Get the schooner and I'll drink it. This lot don't look like they're going to have protected lemons.' He winks at me. He's hamming it up, and I don't think anyone's going to appreciate the performance.

'Remember you're driving, Pete,' I say.

'Could you just try to loosen-off, babe?' he says. 'Just for a bit?' And he smooches me on the cheek.

I look around the bar. There's not a single woman in here. It's all white fellas, thumbing through papers, staring at the large plasma screen fixed to the wall, or staring straight at me. There's no space at any of the tables, so I try to perch on a bar stool. It's not an elegant procedure, now I'm so big. One bloke, his red hair flattened to his head with sweat, keeps on staring the whole time as I clamber up.

Pete hands me the schooner. I suppose I'm meant to pretend to sip it. I put it down on the bar. Pete's grinning like an idiot, turning this way and that, nodding at these drunk strangers. Pete's always been good at making friends. He's an affable bugger, you might say. He's got his guitar, he likes a drink and a smoke, he'll chat to anyone. He says I'm closed up, says I've gotten even more introverted these

9

last few years. I suppose it's true. I don't try to make friends anymore. In fact, most of my friends feel like accidents I should have avoided: new ones used to appear after drunken nights out, like those bruises you can't remember how you got. You inspect them the next morning, trying to remember something best forgotten, and then hope they'll fade quickly.

'G'day,' Pete says to the man who's leaning over a paper next to him at the bar. 'You from round here? We're brand new. Fresh in last night.' Pete's used to his openness winning people over in the city, but the man doesn't look up for a while and it feels like the rules are different out here.

When the man does respond, he stares past Pete and straight at me. 'That right?' he says. 'Not ferals, are ya?'

Pete laughs; the man doesn't. 'No! We're fixed up in a place at the edge of town. After a change of scenery, is all,' Pete says. 'We've come down from the city. Best off out of it with a little fella on the way.' He thumbs in my direction.

'That right?' says the man again. He speaks slowly. His skin is creased around his eyes – creased within a normal range, I'd say – and it stretches tight, chestnut-brown, across his cheek bones. 'Thought you'd get away from it all, I reckon. You'd best not have bothered. Abos. Stacks of 'em out here. Health service can't cope, social services can't cope.' The man picks up his glass, swills it, raises a toast in my general direction. 'And you thought you'd come put some extra strain on the few doctors we've got with that sprog, did ya? Got four myself,' the man says. 'I wouldn't have 'em again, but. Dirty little buggers. Youngest one, if you leave him alone, he'll eat shit. No word of a lie. Found him face down in his brother's nappy, didn't I? Never heard the end of it. No one warns you about that. Little bastards the lot of them.' He drains his pint and puts the glass down on the bar. 'Bloody reckless having them now, with everything that's going on, if you ask me,' he says.

'Well, mate,' Pete says, still smiling sweetly. 'I don't think anyone did ask you.' He turns back to me. 'Bloody bogan,' he says, loud enough for the man to hear. 'Ignore him.'

'Shut up,' I mouth at Pete. 'We're bloody bogans, you know.' We've had this fight before, a hundred times. We grew up on St Paul's, a big public-housing estate in the city. Just because we got away doesn't mean we're not trash too.

'Nah, babe,' Pete says. 'We're not like this fucker.'

The man bangs his empty glass on the bar and jostles Pete on his way past. 'It's a small place, this, *mate*,' he says, dragging his shoulder against Pete's back. 'Not like your city. I'll be seeing you.'

Pete tries to make light of it. Cracks a few jokes about small communities in the mountains. Says that the bloke's four children are probably half-sheep. After a while he strikes up a conversation with the two blokes on the other side of us. They talk about the footie for a while and then about home brew. One of them is making beer in his spare

11

room. Pete tells them he plays guitar and they talk for a long time about recording software, and eventually they invite Pete over. One of them scribbles an address on a piece of paper.

'Ta, mate,' Pete says. 'Gotta piss.' He kisses my forehead on his way to the lavs. 'See,' he whispers, 'they're not all bad.'

When Pete's gone, one of the men leans over to me. Paulie, he's called. He's young and sharp-featured. His hair is the colour of coney fur, slicked back behind his ears. His fingertips are yellow from nicotine, and some of his teeth are caramelised with booze and god knows what else. He has the same look as some of Pete's friends from St Paul's, boys who are plagued by malicious boredom. Cleverness turned to spite. There's a sneer across his face, and when he talks I know that he's going to try to provoke me: 'So, darl,' he says. 'Your old man. Where's he from? Wogs, are ya?'

I eyeball the two of them. 'He's second-generation Greek,' I say. 'There a problem here? You want to make something of that?'

'No problem, love, simmer down,' says Paulie. 'Just interested. Bloody firecracker we've got here.' His mate murmurs something and they both laugh.

When Pete gets back he's pathetically pally with them. He can't wait to record some tunes with them, he can't wait to try their toxic home brew, he can't wait to see their shoddy bloody houses.

'We need to go,' I say.

'Alright, love,' he says. '*Hormones*,' he mouths at them and they titter. 'Catch yous later.'

When we get out onto the street there are a few more people about, but it's quiet still. The glare is bright, even though the shadows are lengthening now. I watch an older couple on the other side of the street: their shadows lean back from them, elongated across the pavement. I feel light headed and I can see all the little floaters in my eyes dancing about, like static on an old telly screen.

'I really need something to drink,' I say. 'I'm dehydrated.' We find a food-mart that's open, down at the bottom of the street, on the corner. I sit down with a carton of juice in the shade outside while Pete gets the essentials: protected eggs and bread, protected indoor-reared meat, beer.

'They're selling loads of unprotected stuff,' he says when he comes out with a carrier bag full. 'It's dirt cheap.'

'We're not eating it,' I say.

'I'm just saying,' Pete says, 'No one has proved anything. All this protected food is probably a racket, if you ask me. I bet we're paying a bloody fortune for no reason.'

'I don't care,' I say. 'We're not eating it.'

As we walk back to the car, we pass a blackfella sitting in the shade in front of one of the empty shops. He's busking. At least I think he is. He's not wearing any shoes and he's playing on a wooden whistle, but there's no sign asking for money, no hat out for coins. I glance down at his feet. Something's not right. We keep on walking and I glance back.

'Bloody hell,' I say to Pete. 'Look at that fella's feet. Can you see?'

We're already a way past him now and Pete hooks his arms through mine, keeping me moving.

'I have no intention of looking at that bloke's feet,' Pete says.

'Wait up. I think he's…' I look back again but we're too far away to see anything clearly now. 'I think I saw…'

'Oh, let me guess what you think you saw. Chri'sake, babe, give it a rest will ya? What was the point of us coming out here if you're going to keep this up? We agreed, didn't we? Look how beautiful it is out here. Smell how clean it is.'

We're back at the car now and Pete inhales theatrically. He turns his head to stare up at the sky. I follow his gaze: the sky is clear and blue, just a few thin clouds drifting above the mountains in the distance. The moon is already high; it's full and round at one side but one-third is missing at the other side, taken up by a curve of blue. It looks as though the moon is made of the same wispy stuff as the clouds and has burnt clean away in the heat.

'Let's get back,' Pete says. He pulls me close and kisses the top of my head. 'There's nothing to worry about out here, Ali,' he says. 'Remember: fresh start.'

* * *

I remember, instead, when my skin seemed like magic. We're in the car driving back to the new house and Pete's singing along to something on the stereo as he drives and I'm looking at my fingers, at the tiny scuffs of skin around a nail where I've caught the cuticle with my teeth and sheared away a stretch of it. There are three pinpricks of old blood, just below the nail bed, and the skin around them is roughed up in tiny bristles. That skin must be dead. And in a few days the pinpricks of blood will be completely gone. The top layer of my skin will have secretly, magically, crept across the tiny wounds, knitting itself back together again. Your skin is ever so clever, my mother used to say when I was a child and had cut myself: it's like a layer of magic all around you. When I fell down the steps at school and cut my knees badly, jewelled with blood and grit, she picked the wounds clean with tweezers, wiped each one with something that stung so sharp it made me giddy, and then she covered me in fabric sticking plaster. In three nights' time, we'll check again, she said, and we did, we checked together, sitting on the edge of my bed, and it was like lifting the lid on an experiment. The first time we looked, the wounds were still wet, but a few days later even the worst of the cuts was starting to heal, the flesh beneath dulled to purple, the skin settling back into a dry gauze of grazes. In another few days, both knees had scabbed over, and then, a few weeks down the line – nothing, no sign of anything, nothing left of the injury at all. My knees had sealed back over, the new skin clean and soft and supple. It made me think of my skin as a silvery fabric that fluttered around me in the night, netting me back together. Just look at my arms! my mother had said, when my wounds were still fresh. She worked in a vet's surgery back then: an auxiliary who handed cats and dogs into their cages every day. Wrist to elbow she was always covered in scratches, and her hands were often bruised and bloody from cat bites. This one, she said, drawing my finger all the way along a long, thin graze, this one was nasty. A big old Tom caught his claw in me like a hook and unzipped me all the way along my arm. Ugh, I said, and thought of her being unzipped, her skin like a suit, leaving what behind? Not a person, not a person under there, just some awful hot, veiny mess. Ugh. But look, she said, it's almost healed. You can hardly feel it now. She ran my finger up and down the scratch, so thin now that I could barely find its teeth. That's how clever your skin is, she said, it makes the bad things disappear.

There was a girl at school got burned by a firework. Everyone knew the story: it had crackled its way round the schoolyard. A rocket had gone off in the Bardis' backyard on New Year's Eve, only it had fallen on its side after Mr Bardi lit the fuse, spinning out of control, bouncing off the walls, and chasing the whole family back into the house. Then it burst in through the window, smashing glass everywhere and spearing Leena in the thigh. She was the prettiest, liveliest girl in our class; dark-skinned and tall, her long limbs were always draped around her friends, comforting them, drawing them in close. Afterwards, for a long while, she was jittery. She got thin and withdrawn, and startled at loud noises in the playground. You could see the whites of her eyes all of the time. But, eventually, we saw her skin work its magic. They gave her grafts, taking flesh from her buttocks and plying it back into her thigh. In PE we caught glimpses of the large cotton pads that she wore under her school skirt and speculated eagerly on what was underneath. And when the day came, a year or so later, that the pads were gone, we gathered around her in silence. She lifted her skirt, slowly, coquettishly, and showed us the magic. Her dark skin gleamed: her outer thigh curved ever so slightly inwards where it had once bowed, but the skin had meshed back together, a pale lattice of new scars. She lowered her skirt, smiled shyly, laced her arm around her best friend's neck again.

That was the old magic. But we live in new times. I can't depend on the old magic of skin, on the old secrets of healing. Our skin is a hex on us now: it turns our bodies to puffs of smoke, choking out their own fires.

These are the thoughts I'm not meant to have. This is what Pete wants us to leave behind.

'Here we are, babe.' Pete swings the car up in front of the house. Our house, our Mountain View. 'Welcome home.'

I feel the tiny scuffs of skin around my nail; I press them down with my thumb and I will them to mend quick and clean. Oh lord, keep me safe from harm. Oh lord, keep me safe from my skin.

II

THE next morning it's my job to go register at the doctors' while Pete carries on with the unpacking. We found a surgery and marked it on the map before we came out here – which is lucky, because it'll be at least a week before we get a phone-line and we still can't get reception on either of our mobiles. I get into the car to drive to Lakoomba. I have to push the seat back and I need to hold my arms at a weird angle to accommodate my stomach. I haven't driven since I got this big. The bump feels so prominent, so precarious behind the wheel. What happens if I need to brake suddenly? Pete says I'm more robust than I know, that any baby of ours will be made of stern stuff. Still, when I glance down at my stomach, at its improbable roundness, I can't help thinking of overripe objects splitting and spoiling: of swollen fruit softening to mush, of big, soft egg-yolks bleeding yellow across a plate, of a torn jellyfish I once saw on the beach, spilling out her oily innards. Pete says fixating on things that might happen only makes life worse. But I've seen things that Pete hasn't, the sorts of things that flash back to you, unbidden, like bright lights that score through the darkness even after you shut your eyes. It's not easy to forget these things.

I drive slowly, I drive so slowly that braking would hardly be noticeable, and I get a good look at the streets that lead into town. There's one house that's probably walking distance from ours, half-an-hour at a push. It's a similar construction to Mountain View: square, with a pitched, tiled roof, a verandah and a large garden. It's no longer white: the paint has almost entirely peeled away and the wood underneath is now grey and splitting in places. The garden is overgrown, and a longhaired cat, fat and shabby, sunbathes on the front porch. After this house there are no others for a while and the road banks steeply down into the valley bottom. There's a clear view of the mountains from here. The nearest edge is made of jagged, golden rocks, a deadly-looking set of giant stalagmites. At the foot of this crop, the dense green of the eucalypt begins. And beyond the green sprawl of the valley the mountains really are blue, shading away into the dark, indigo distance. Trying to see that far feels like trying to peer back through time. My eyes strain and I have to look back at the road. The mountains mark the beginning of the forest. Nearly four thousand miles of it, some of it still unmapped.

Swamps and heathlands and rainforest and hidden woods full of relic species. That's what they call them: Wollemia trees, extinct everywhere else in the world, still grow in pockets here, relics from millions of years back when the continent was still one landmass. No one's allowed to visit the most ancient trees, in case they bring modern bugs, and their location is kept secret. If anywhere's still clean, Pete says, it's here. The forest will clean the air.

On the outskirts of town there are more houses. I can see that this used to be a nice place to live. There are clusters of pretty, red-roofed cottages on the hillside. They look almost Mediterranean. When you get closer up, they're no longer so picturesque. There are cracked panes, slipped tiles, more splitting wood. This used to be a tourist town, before the summers got so ferocious. At the very edge of town there's an area of run-down shacks. It's not quite a shanty, but it's not far off. The doctors' surgery is just beyond here, on a corner where the shacks meet the shops that signal the start of the town centre: a couple of mini-marts, a drug store, a discount t-shirt shop that has made a temporary home in an abandoned seafood restaurant. I park the car. At least there are a few more people around today. I inspect them from behind my sunnies. I'd imagined that out here people would seem less frazzled, less worn-down than in the city. Maybe it's the heat today; the people I pass seem even more broken than back home. There's a dark-skinned woman carrying a crying child; her skin is oily and the soft spots under her eyes have sunk inwards, making her face look as though it's collapsing with tiredness. Two old, tanned, white men walk together towards me. One is bow legged and evidently in pain; the other spits as he passes by. Their clothes are smeared with dirt and they smell of fried food and sweat.

When I reach the doctors' surgery, there are several notices pinned to the door, covering older notices. Some of them are hand-written, scrawled in felt-tip. 'Emergencies only. For routine medical issues, visit the pharmacy on Freelander Ave.' When I push open the door, the waiting area is chocka. There's a queue down the left-hand side of the room, composed of antsy, jiggling people. Others sit on a crescent of chairs at the right-hand side of the room. The heat is unbearable. I hear crying and turn to see a young boy sitting on one of the chairs. He's covering his ears with his hands and he's keening like a dog. While I'm staring at the boy, a nurse appears alongside me and takes hold of my elbow.

'How far along are you?' she asks.

'Thirty-six weeks,' I say. 'Actually, almost thirty-seven.'

'Ok,' she says. 'You're in the high-risk category. I can take you straight past the queue to see the doctor. Where are your symptoms?'

'Symptoms?' I say. 'What do you mean? I've come to register. I– '

She pulls up. 'If you're not symptomatic you need to leave right away,' she says. 'I suppose you didn't see the signs on the door?'

She's walking me out now, like a bouncer. I glance over my shoulder, back to the crying boy. He's pressing against his ears with the flats of his palms, gritting his teeth.

The nurse helps me through the door, ejecting me onto the pavement. Her face is stony: she's used to reprimanding people. 'You can't take up space in here,' she says. 'We're full. Folk keep passing out in the heat.'

'But I've just moved here,' I say. 'I need to register before the birth. I need a midwife.'

The nurse pauses and looks at me a little more kindly. Her blonde hair is swept back into a bun. Her eyeliner has turned fudgey in the heat and it's working its way into the creases around her eyes. She wipes the sweat that's collecting on her forehead back into her hair. 'Is it your first?' she asks.

'Yes,' I say.

'Why in God's name have you come out here?'

'Fresh start,' I say, softly. I don't know if she hears me. 'What did you mean, symptoms?' I ask, trying not to panic. 'Do you mean that all those people in there have symptoms of– ,' I can feel the sting of bile at the bottom of my throat. It's probably just heartburn – it's happened a few times since I've got this big – though I feel like I might be sick.

'Listen,' she says. 'We're only doing emergency services

from this surgery now. Nowhere that I know is registering regular patients. The midwives are flat out, dealing with... complications. Did you go to antenatal classes?'

'Yes,' I say. We attended classes back in the city. Pete had mostly made jokes and flirted with the instructor. I'd assiduously taken notes, but I knew even then that the scant physical details and jolly, convivial atmosphere of the group wasn't any real sort of preparation. Measured breathing and lavender oil for the 'discomfort'? I've been in maternity wards. I've seen the stirrups and the episiotomy scissors and the epidural needles and the scalpels. These places smell more like slaughterhouses than the afternoon spa-trip the instructor was preparing us for.

'Well, you'll know how to recognise labour then,' the nurse says. 'Once you get established, your partner needs to drive you to the hospital. It's a little over an hour from here.' I guess I must look crestfallen, because she says, 'If you've got a partner?'

'Yes,' I say.

'And a car?' she asks.

'Yes.'

'And were there any early risk factors or complications in your pregnancy?'

'No.'

'Then just thank your lucky stars. Make sure you ring the hospital as soon as you get going, in case they don't have beds. They won't admit you if they're full with emergencies. If you ring and they're full, they'll tell you where to present instead. The next hospital along is an hour-and-a-half away.'

'Our birth plan was for a home birth,' I say, 'so I need a midwife.'

'Home birth?' she says, and she laughs out loud. 'And you're primigravida? It's your first pregnancy? And you're over an hour from the nearest hospital and all of *this* is going on?'

'What do you mean, "all of this"? Are all those people symptomatic with cutis?' Her face turns downwards, severe again, so I try another tack. 'Listen, I saw some cases in the city. I work for the Department of Housing. I know that something is going on, that it's more serious than they're letting on. My partner won't believe me. Thinks I'm exaggerating things. Is it happening out here, too?'

'Listen,' she says, looking me up and down. I made an effort today: a long maternity dress, a brush through my hair, some face-lotion and mascara. Perhaps I look reasonable. 'You can find all the official advice online. There have been fewer cases out here, up to now. But there are fewer medical staff, too, and we're not getting any extra support, you can be sure of that. We're in what they call a "rapidly changing situation". I've got to go. There are people in here who need my help right now.'

'When you said I was "high-risk" because I was pregnant,

did you mean at higher-risk of cutis symptoms, or that the symptoms are more dangerous?' I ask. And then, 'What does it mean, "a rapidly changing situation"? Does that mean things are getting worse?'

She turns away and closes the door to the surgery behind her.

I sit in the car for a while and rest my head against the steering wheel. Even the plastic is clammy. If we were back in the city I'd be recording this now, racing home to put the details into my files: location, number of suspected cases, exact words of medical practitioner. I'd be checking the internet for clues of other cases in the area and I'd be posting on my blog: 'Central Lakoomba: New cases suspected. Medical staff refuse to admit routine patients.' My conspiracy files, Pete calls them. I'm not supposed to be recording this stuff anymore. And I'm definitely not supposed to be blogging about it. Pete says it's ghoulish and obsessive and that the stress of thinking about it must be bad for the baby. And it's true that it almost cost me my job. So we came to this agreement: we'd get out here, to Lakoomba, and I'd start from scratch, we'd both start from scratch. I'd leave behind my misdemeanours, Pete would leave behind his, and we'd try to make something new together. But how can I leave it behind if it's out here too? One day, someone's going to want to know how this all played out, how they tried to cover it up. And my records, at least, will be there for them.

I drive back from Lakoomba more quickly than I drove out, and when I get back to the house I'm sick in the kitchen sink. My gullet stings for a while afterwards, so I rinse out my mouth and gulp down a couple of glasses of water. I was lucky in the early stages of the pregnancy, I guess, and was hardly sick at all. Maybe these things can start to happen in the later stages? Or perhaps this is something else? The water still tastes strange to me out here. I need to ask Pete to check on the paperwork for the pump, make sure the water's filtered, make sure it's not making us sick. I feel a flutter of panic. Without the internet there might be no way for me to obsess over what's happening in the city; but there's also no way to check what's normal at this stage in the pregnancy. I'll ask Pete to drive somewhere he can get reception later on, so that he can ask his mum. There's no need to panic, that's what Pete will say. The nurse said I'd be fine and she's a medical professional. But I can't help thinking of the boy with the flats of his palms over his ears. What was happening to him? What was happening to the skin of his ears? A rapidly changing situation, the nurse said. I wash my hands and dampen my hair and cheeks with water. I can feel that my skin's unusually hot. It's as I'm standing over the sink, resting my weight on its edges, that I notice something out in the garden: some sort of movement. I survey the backyard through the kitchen window. There it is again, a flutter at the edge of the bushes. I move over to the door and step carefully out onto the verandah. Then I sink down low, squatting at the edge of the wooden platform and resting my weight on its lip. I sit very still. I don't have to wait long and then there it is again: a small disturbance in the clump of bottlebrush at the edge of the flower border. The yellow, fuzzy heads of the flowers shake violently until, gradually, the movement subsides. There's no breeze, but the bulbs of yellow are still swaying gently. What's in there? It must be something small and quick. We haven't seen anything wild in the city for such a long time. I can feel my heart beating quickly in my chest, stupidly excited at the prospect of seeing something feral. People said that animals were surviving better out here, creatures that have long disappeared back home. Perhaps it's true then, perhaps this is the proof: things are thriving out here, so the air must be cleaner. Maybe it's a bandicoot? I haven't seen one since I was small child and they used to visit our backyard on rare, magical evenings. Mum would fetch torches and we would watch them using their long, furry noses to root around for insects at the edges of the flower beds. But bandicoots forage at night. Whatever this is, it's a daytime critter. It's too small to be dangerous – far too small to be a dingo, for instance. And it's too big to be poisonous: no brown snake or funnel-web spider or bull ant could cause this kind of shaking. I carry on sitting, quiet and still, waiting for something alive to reveal itself. There's another couple of rounds of shaking and then I catch a glimpse of it: the shaking's caused by the skittish movements of a small bird. It's not quite as exciting as I was hoping for but, still, birds are rare enough in the city these days. There's the flutter of a wing and then nothing for a while longer. What can it be doing in there? Perhaps it's found some tasty but resistant morsel. Perhaps it's engaged in a protracted struggle with a particularly tenacious worm. Suddenly, the bird spins itself out of the bush and into the open. It spins itself onto the lawn, and then stands still and flaps its wings. Not in a taking-off kind of way; more in a shake-down kind of a way. It's a pretty little thing: sleek amber feathers on its body, which shade into gold on its back and look greenish on its belly; a black head with little white patches on its cheeks. A honey-eater, I think, with its long, sharp, nectar-drinking beak. I haven't seen one in years. I want to run and get Pete from upstairs, but if I move I might frighten it away. The bird stands entirely still for a few seconds more. And then it spins on the ground again and flutters its wings. I've never seen a bird move like this. It's as though it's using its wings to sweep the area around it, or else to show-off, in a kind of dance. Maybe it's some sort of courtship ritual. But it's the wrong time of year, surely, and I scan the area for other birds: there's nothing to see. The bird wheels around again, flutters its wings in an extended circle around its own body. Little by little, it's moving closer and closer to me. I watch it perform this strange ritual a few more times, as it intermittently spins itself towards the verandah. Between spins it keeps its wings held out at a battish angle. It's as though it's poised for movement at any moment, concentrating intensely even while it rests.

It's about five feet away when I realise that, despite its spinning, when it comes to a rest there's a remarkable stillness to the bird. No movement at all. None of those jerky, skittish little tics that birds, always watching for danger, usually have. And there's no movement in the bird's eyes at all. Just a dead stillness. The bird spins again and when it comes to a stop, I stare at it hard. It's only a couple of feet away now. Its head is angled towards me, but it doesn't seem to see me. It looks as though the bird's eyes are closed, though I know this can't be possible, that its eyelids don't work this way. I remember the weirdness of bird eyes, from when we used to see them in my mother's backyard. I remember her telling me that they don't blink, exactly: sight is too important to them. She must've known something about birds by the end of her stint at the vet's: she'd taken care of parrots, and parakeets, and birds of prey. Their eyelids were lubricated by a nictitating membrane, she told me proudly in the backyard one morning, pronouncing the strange words carefully. Nictitating membrane: a third eyelid that sweeps across the eyeball from the side or the bottom. But this bird's eyes *look* closed: there's dark grey skin covering them with the consistency of scuffed suede. The bird makes one more turn towards me, and then it's so close that I get a really good look and then I'm sure of it: the bird can't open its eyes. The eyelid skin makes a dome, fused over the place where the bright little eyes should be. It makes me think of baby birds, the thin, orange skin that covers the glowing blue bulbs of their eyes if they hatch prematurely. This bird's skin is thick and over-developed. Its eyes look reptilian: dry and powdery. And there's no sign of anything below the skin, no latent flinch towards opening. The bird's eyes have been completely sealed over. And now the spinning begins to make a kind of sense: it's blindly twirling, sweeping around with its wings, trying to work out where it is. I stand straight up and I gasp. I need to get more air. I try not to let the fear inside me escape into sound. My sudden movement must be loud enough to scare the bird anyway. It spins around several times in a panicked flurry and then it takes off into the sky. It hits the branches of the peppermint at the bottom of the garden, calling out a high distress-note, and then it plummets, swooping towards the valley, falling out of sight.

We're sitting at the kitchen table and I can't stop my hands from shaking. The tremor runs all the way through my wrists up into my elbows. I grip my hands together and squeeze them hard between my thighs until I can't feel anything except my knuckles digging into the soft flesh there.

'You've been through a lot,' Pete says, 'we both know that.' He's making a cup of tea for me and cracking open a beer for himself. 'But, Alice, I think what you've been through, it affects how you see things sometimes.' He's speaking slowly and very deliberately, as though I'm a small child to whom he's explaining complicated adult business. He puts the tea down in front of me and some of the tan liquid sloshes up and over the lip of the cup, running away down the sleek porcelain edge and disappearing into the grain of the wooden table. That's the thing about Pete: he doesn't notice details like this. He doesn't care about the little things and he doesn't realise that they matter, that they can add up to bigger things.

He sits down beside me and squeezes my arm, as though the problem is with me, rather than out there, in the sky and in the water and in the birds and in everything around us.

'There's never been a report of birds having symptoms, not even in the city, has there?' he says. He swigs on his beer, leans back in his chair. 'Look, that bird could have come from anywhere. So maybe you're right. Maybe there was something wrong with its eyes. But that could be caused by anything! It could be congenital. It could be some kind of disease. It could have flown in from anywhere and brought some kind of new bird flu with it.'

'It was an adult bird, Pete,' I say, trying to sound calm and reasonable, though my voice is breathless and whiny, even to my own ears. 'There's no way it could have survived if it was born that way. And it couldn't have flown any distance in that state. It must have happened recently, so it must have happened here.'

Pete puts his bottle down on the table. 'Alice, you're assuming things that you can't know for sure,' he says. 'You're imagining it everywhere, making inferences. I get it, babe, I really do. What you went through with your mum. It's a classic stress response. You're repeating the whole thing in your head, making it appear again and again. But that doesn't mean it's really happening. You need to think about the future, about this little one.' He rubs the top of my stomach in the way that you might ruffle the fur on a dog's head. I feel static prickle across my dress. 'That's what we agreed. We're leaving all this behind us. Right? Fresh start?'

'I'm telling you exactly what I saw,' I say. 'You just don't want to listen. It's like yesterday in town. That bloke, sitting on the street, I told you there was something wrong with his feet and you didn't even want to look. I'm not seeing things – you're refusing to look out there, to see what's really going on.' I'm gesticulating now, waving my right hand wildly in the direction of the verandah. My voice has gone funny. I'm not going to cry. I am not going to cry. It's just the tremor, it's all the way through me now.

Pete stands up. He cradles my head in his hands and pushes my face against his stomach. 'Shhh, babe,' he says. 'You're alright. Everything's going to be alright.' For a moment I breathe him in and I forget where we are: I shut my eyes and let myself be cocooned into Pete's body. Since we were kids, Pete and I have always retreated into one another like this. We grew up next door to each other, fooled around when we were teenagers. We tried to be together after college, which was a disaster. And then for years afterwards, whenever we were homesick or feeling lost, whenever relationships ended, whenever we were grieving, we always found one another. It was my mother dying that took me back to him again this time; and then I fell pregnant, and that means that we're doing things properly now, Pete says, like we always should have.

There's a reason we didn't 'do things properly'. Pete likes to forget that we've tried this before, that it wasn't me who screwed things up the first time. I'm breathing into his t-shirt, the soft cotton sucking against my nose and mouth. I try to relax, I try to remember what it was like to feel safe with Pete, but I can't help it: I start to picture the man's feet, the man sitting on the roadside yesterday. I should have recorded that. Did I see it clearly? Am I remembering it right? The man's skin is dark, creased all over but supple-looking. The man's toes are long, articulated with bulbous bones like arthritic knuckles. It's the ends of his toes where things get strange: there should have been nails there, ten blunt bits of pale, ridged protein, shiny, or made dull with dirt. Instead, I can only see more skin: the dark, soft material curves around the end of each toe, the man's nails swallowed up. I'm sure of it. And if I can see it again so clearly, surely I can't have made this up, I can't have imagined it. I can't get enough air. I'm hyperventilating against Pete's t-shirt. The cotton mixes with his scent and it's filling my mouth, covering my nose. I lash out at Pete, pushing him away.

'I can't breathe,' I say, 'get the fuck off me,' and Pete stumbles backwards.

We're in bed together, in our new bedroom. It's late and Pete's already asleep, but the sky is still alive with the summer day – a dark, vivid blue – and I'm still agitated. I can't stop thinking about the bird; and then I can't stop thinking about the city, remembering all of the things that I've recorded in my files.

The very first day of it, the day it all began, started out ordinarily enough. It was hot and, for once, clear. No smog at all. I woke early and I walked to work from my bedsit in the old town and I stood on the harbour bridge, pausing for a long moment. Taking the air, my mother used to call it, and I really did take in that clean, clear air, breathing it deeply, gulping it in, turning to see the view. There were a number of ways I could get to work and I varied them, depending on my mood, the severity of my hangover, the density of the smog. This was a day for walking, for watching the glittering sea, for slicing through the different sections of town before I landed at my desk, to sit under the low ceiling and rattling air-con. That moment on the bridge: have I once breathed so deeply since? The sky was bright blue, not a cloud in it, the air was warm and still fresh, the harbour was busy with little commuter boats crossing the bay. There were no birds in the sky, but things still felt hopeful. I'm sure they did, I'm sure there was still hope then. I can just about remember it, hopefulness. I know that my body felt light and restless; my stomach was empty in that good, yearning way, the way that drives you on. I might have put my hands on my waist: I might have felt my own tautness, my compact density; I was full of myself, back then, and only myself. I looked out across the harbour. If I were to fall from the bridge, I felt that I would float, lifted on the thermals, buoyed-up by my own energy.

I arrived at work, poured out my cereal, began to process my cases. There was a kind of carnival atmosphere in the office: these bright, clear days were increasingly rare. I remember odd details: Kimmy, my boss, was wearing a jumpsuit with a garish, tropical pattern. Tony was making plans to take his kids to the beach after work: he would pack a picnic and take the boat across the harbour and show them how you could see all the way to the city while you made sand-pies when the sky was clear. Doreen says that her lungs are clear today and that she hasn't had to use her eye drops – she keeps on whistling. We're all taking things a bit easier than usual and I can see that Mandy, at the desk next to me, is intermittently clicking on sites for scuba-diving holidays and night-school courses in DJing. She's planning alternative lives; the clear skies made these things feel possible.

By mid-morning, Kimmy was pacing around, dashing in and out of the office, and swearing under her breath a lot, which wasn't so unusual. By mid-afternoon, her agitation had built to a kind of crisis and she planted herself in the middle of the office, legs akimbo, clapping her hands. 'Listen up, ladies and gents, there's something I need you all to take a look at. I've sent you a preview, front page of tomorrow's Herald. You lucky buggers. Go ahead, read through it.' She remained standing in the centre of the room, arms folded. We all turned back to our terminals and clicked through to the article. 'Sealed-In By His Own Skin?' the headline ran. I skimmed through it, alighting on the main points. I'd pour over it later that evening, reading it again and again, returning to it compulsively on my phone in the sleepless early hours. A homeless man had been found dead. It seemed that he'd been sheltering at the edge of the big rubbish tip on the outskirts of the city; his body was found in the midst of the trash. And it's a wonder he was found at all, really; the report made it clear that he'd hidden himself pretty effectively, improvising some sort of shelter from large sheaths of plastic. Cause of death was thought to be suffocation. He was near covered in rubbish. This wasn't a straight-forward death-by-interment-in-debris. That might have made the news, but certainly not the front page. The men who found the body were claiming something much stranger.

I've often thought about those two men working together on the morning that they found the body. What would it have been like to have seen the very first symptomatic in the city, with no clue about what you were witnessing? This is how I picture it: one of the men is operating a large bulldozer, driving it across the dump to compact the waste. The other is on foot, walking along the road that runs through the site, slightly ahead of the vehicle, scouting for anything that might cause the bulldozer any problems. When they get to a far corner of the site, Barry Patton, the walker, spots something slightly unusual. There's a regular irregularity to the surface of the rubbish, ordinarily, an averaging of the shambles of discarded objects. On a day like this – overcast, the clouds curdling in the heat of the sky like roiling, grey-gold fudge – Barry looks out across the regular, irregular surface of the rubbish and it makes him think of different things, none of them pleasant: it makes him think of a shipwreck, a broken vessel smashed to pieces, and the rubbish is the new, bobbing surface of a sea of ruined objects; it makes him think of the demolition sites he used to work on, of a building, half-knocked down, its outer walls smashed away, each floor exposed, everything spilling out like shredded paper, and then, finally, collapsed into a rocky, metallic stew, simmering down to dust; it makes him think of mass graves, of bodies leafing over one another, inert but still producing warmth and movement and odour as they decompose, caving into one another. All of these surfaces share the same levelled, gently undulating chaos of the dump. But here, here in the corner of the dump, is something different. Larger pieces of plastic are collected together in one place (already this is unusual – similar objects don't usually remain so close to one another), and some of them have been placed together, rising above the rest of the mess, creating a small triangle. It looks like a shanty construction of some kind.

Barry whistles loudly, to get the bulldozer driver's attention, flagging him to stop, and then immediately regrets removing his mask to put his fingers in his mouth: they taste of soil and something worse, and the sour smell of the tip still has the power to surprise him. He carries on waving, shouts to his workmate, 'Stop, stop, stop.' The machine grinds to a halt and its blade stutters in mid-air, freezing half-way through its cycle. Mike jumps down from the cab. 'What is it, mate?'

'There's something in that corner,' Barry shouts back, jumping up onto the rubbish mound and starting to make his way across.

'Watch your step,' Mike says, 'hasn't been compressed in a few days.'

When Barry gets to the corner, to the corrugated plastic sheeting secured against the embankment that forms the edge of the dump, he sees a pair of boots. At first this doesn't strike him as so very strange. His mind has adapted to anomalous sights. Barry is in charge of covering operations, spreading soil across the rubbish each evening after compaction. He's used to seeing odd things, half-compressed, disappearing under the dirt: a wedding dress, folding its own netting away; a sofa haemorrhaging its stuffing; a distorted doll's head seeming, briefly, to reveal a child's pained face, before it is turned under the earth. So the boots are not so strange to Barry, at first. What is odd is their being together. And what is even odder is their being upright, placed on top of the rubbish. Barry is right beside the plastic shack now, and he starts with the uppermost piece of plastic. It's been secured somehow, but with a little pressure it comes away. The structure is not high: he's looking down into it now, as though he's taken off the top of a dog kennel. It's not easy to see at first: the floor of the shack is made of rubbish, a mess of compressed plastic and polythene. He fleetingly sees a man's face. It doesn't register, not yet. It's not a face, it can't be a man's face. He sees the sandy hair, dark with oil and filth. He sees the beard, frayed and yellowish at the edges. He sees the dark, creased places where the eyes are closed, the skin lucent with grease. There are flies buzzing, there are flies rising as he moves to peer in closer. As hard as he stares, he cannot make a mouth or nose appear. Instead, he sees whitish sinews, binding the lower lip up to the top lip, filling in the space where the man's nostrils should be. The skin has made gristled, solid scars where a face's features should be. The texture of them makes Barry think of suet, and then of maggots. Is this some kind of weird decomposition? Is it mangled plastic? Is it something caught on the man's face? It must be. The strangeness of the scene draws him in, stops him turning away from the body in repulsion as he otherwise might. He reaches down with a gloved hand. He draws his thick, rubberised fingertips across the place the mouth should be. There's no movement. It's as though the man has had a bodged skin graft, fusing his lips together. It's as though he's wearing a breathing mask, Barry thinks, a mask made of... his own skin.

'Don't come over here,' he shouts to Mike. 'Do not come over here.'

I'm elaborating, of course, like I always do when I think about these things late at night. In the initial news report there were fewer details of this discovery; but there was a gory artist's impression, a pencil sketch of a man's face with sinewy flesh eating-up the lower portion. The angle of the

41

man's head in the picture even made it look as though he was struggling against his skin, chin tilted up, eyes locked shut in agony. It looked like a mock-up for a new comic-book mutant. The report included medical speculations as well as the dump-workers' statements: one expert suggested that, if the men's reports were true, the dead man's appearance was likely to be the result of an extremely rare skin condition left untreated. A massive haemangioma, or even a very extreme case of warts, could cause it to look to the untrained eye as though the mouth and nose had been covered over in skin. *Cutis laxa*, a chronic lack of elastin in the skin, could cause a person's skin to droop, which could, again, make it appear that the mouth and nose had been covered in skin. This was likely to be a tragic case of under-diagnosis or the sufferer avoiding medical treatment, according to one of the experts consulted for the piece. But another expert, a Professor at the School of Tropical Medicine, suggested a different possible cause. He was hearing of similar reports in several countries, he claimed: we could, in fact, be witnessing the emergence of a new condition. This condition might, he suggested, be similar in mechanism to an auto-immune disease: a potentially deadly, mis-directed defence response. The skin in these newly reported cases was acting in aberrant ways, knitting together in disastrous patterns: might it be, he speculated, that the skin was attempting to protect the body from dangerous environmental pollutants, sealing the body off in the process? The article finished by proposing that toxic substances in the rubbish tip may have triggered some kind of unprecedented defence-response in the man.

The story was going to be big local news. There'd been protests about the dump and its incinerator for months, and the smogs over the city were getting worse and worse. Local groups were already warning that the site was emitting dangerous levels of dioxins far too close to the city, that it was doing god knows what else to the air. 'So,' Kim shouted, when we'd just about had chance to scan the article, 'we'll be in the frigging firing line if we're not careful. I don't want any of you saying a word about this outside the Department. No little off-the-record quips or speculations to ANYONE, nearest and dearest included. They've not confirmed this man's identity, but he's homeless, obvs, so you can bet he's crossed our path at some point. If we've refused him emergency housing, I don't want the spotlight to shift from Waste Disposal to us. So let's hope the press keep the focus on this poor bugger's messed-up face.'

That afternoon, we searched the Department's records for anyone we'd recently seen who might've ended up at the dump. And we identified him, eventually, the city's first known cutis victim: a middle-aged, single man, who'd been out of work for a while and was staying with family. No urgent need for re-housing, his case notes told us. What had we missed when we assessed him? And what am

I missing about cutis right now, back in the city and out here in Lakoomba?

The blue has finally burnt out of the sky, leaving it dark as a fire-pit. Something moves in the dark inside me, kicking me hard between my legs. It's the last thing I feel before I sink into sleep.

III

WE wake with the dawn. The clock says 04:32. There are strange cries out at the edge of the forest: long, falling caws and the chatty clicks of bush crickets. We don't have curtains yet and the morning light falls across the room, bleaching pale strips of the floor. It's going to be another hot one. I can see that Pete is eying me from across the bed, trying to work out if I'm awake and safe to approach. We're being careful with one another. I begin to roll towards him, but I hit my stomach hard against the mattress: I still forget, sometimes, in these first few moments of being awake, that the bump is there. I shuffle more carefully across the mattress until I'm close to him, close enough to smell his warm, salty just-awake scent.

'I'm sorry,' I say. 'I'm sorry about last night. I know you were trying to reassure me.'

He pushes his muzzle into my neck. 'Nah, *I'm* sorry, babe,' he says. 'You've got so much to deal with right now. I get it. You're being super vigilant.' He lays his right arm over the bump and reaches round my back to hold my shoulder. 'It's probably hormonal. A mother tiger thing. We're going to be just fine, Alice.' He kisses me on both eyelids. He used to do this sort of thing and it felt precious: he'd kiss all the vulnerable places where blood and tendons rise too close to the surface, protecting them with the charm of his care; my throat, my wrists, the backs of my knees. But since I saw my mother's body, Pete's careful eyelid kisses feel morbid, like a death rite. His kisses make me think of that ancient Greek tradition of placing coins on the eyes of a corpse.

He takes my face in his hands. 'I need you to stop worrying, Ali, and trust me that we're somewhere safe. We came out here for a good reason. All this panicking, it's not good for you, and it can't be good for the baby.' He kisses me again and then he casts the sheet off his body. He sleeps naked and his dark hair makes a soft, curled pattern, horizontal across his chest and then tapering downwards into a whorl around his cock. 'Right, as we're awake, I'm getting you some protected juice and I'm getting myself some old-fashioned filthy coffee. And then you're going to tell me what happened at the doctors'.' He strides across the room, scratches his right ear, and is gone.

I curl myself around the bump, holding it with both hands. It feels slightly different today. There's a heavy ache around the bottom of it, sharpening into little stabbing jolts, which move downwards into my thighs. Could be a touch of sciatica, I guess. Or the dreaded SPD: I remember a woman at our antenatal class who could barely walk – the bump had pushed her pelvis right apart. I straighten out, try to stretch the feeling away. There's the sickness again, an acidic fizz at the bottom of my gullet. And, of course, I need to pee. I push my face against the pillow, searching for coolness. Then I give up and lumber out of the bed to the loo. The morning already feels close and humid.

When I come back, Pete is sitting up in bed with his coffee. I climb back in beside him.

'I wish you wouldn't,' I say. 'We don't know where that coffee was grown or what it's been sprayed with.'

'Alice,' he says, patiently, 'I've been drinking Greek coffee since I was three years old. There's no problem with coffee.'

'We don't know that,' I say. 'We don't know what's causing it. It could be absolutely anything.'

'Babe, I don't want to argue,' he says. 'Tell me what happened at the doctors' yesterday. Why didn't they register you?'

We had barely spoken after the bird fiasco yesterday. Pete stormed away into the garden. I hyperventilated for a while in the living-room. He tried to make friends later on, coming back in, fixing us dinner. And I tried to eat, but the food tasted strange in my mouth. 'Is this protected?' I'd asked and Pete had sighed. 'Yes,' he said. 'Why don't you tell me what happened at the doctors'?' The tomatoes tasted funny to me, metallic, so I got up and started looking for the packaging. 'What happened at the doctors', Alice? Are you listening to me?' I was going through the bin by this point, convinced he'd not checked the labelling properly, that he'd gone for some cheap stuff and I was eating pesticides. 'Couldn't bloody register, could I? Said they were only dealing with *emergencies*. I know what that means. Cutis. You can bet on it. They wouldn't let me anywhere near a doctor.' I found the plastic wrapping, fished it out and smoothed it on the kitchen counter. The tomatoes did have protected status. Though what about the plastic itself? What if it was the plastic that was transferring chemicals to the fruit? There was no information about the composition of the wrapping itself, just details on the protection level of the tomatoes (*organically grown with 5* protection*). 'Fucksake,' Pete had shouted from the dining table. 'You're impossible when you get like this. You're not the only one affected by this, you know. I'm going to bed.'

So I try to tell him about the doctors' now, in a measured way, so that he won't think I'm exaggerating.

'The doctors' was full,' I say. 'They're not registering any new patients. There were signs all over the door, saying emergencies only. I went in anyway, thinking they might make an exception for pregnancies. But they were completely chocka. Loads of people waiting for surgery.' I think of the little boy again, keening and covering his ears. 'A nurse came and practically frog-marched me off the premises. I had a chat with her outside. She says the hospital will take us when we go into labour, but only if they've got beds. We have to ring ahead of time. There's a hospital an hour away, and another half-an-hour further than that.'

'Fucksake,' Pete says, 'you're kidding?'

'No,' I say. 'Pete, the nurse said it's a *rapidly changing situation*. What do you think that means?'

Pete scowls. 'It means they're bloody hicks and they can't deliver a service properly.'

'I don't know,' I say. 'I'm worried there might be cases out here, things that they're not equipped for. Have you heard from anyone? Have you seen any news?'

'No, babe,' he says. 'You know I can't get reception anywhere around here. We'll be connected soon, but.'

I decide not to say anything more. Nothing he could construe as hysteria. 'I had an idea,' I say, 'yesterday, before all that stuff with the bird.'

'Yeah?' he says.

'I know we get the phone-line in a few days, but it'd be good to know if there's a phone close by. There's a house, not too far down the road. I passed it yesterday. Maybe a half-an-hour walk. Could we go down there? See if they've got a phone? And while we're there you could see if you can get reception.

Give your mum a call. There's a few things I'd like to ask her.'

'Sure,' he says. 'Beaut of an idea. Let me do a few hours work and we'll head down this avo. Be good to meet the neighbours! Babe,' he says, 'I know this is all unsettling. But we'll be sorted in a week's time and we'll be absolutely ready for this little fella.' He strokes my belly and puts his face close up to it. 'Or little Sheila.'

Pete disappears into the makeshift office he's set up in the spare room. He's using a small trestle table, a camping chair, and piles of brochures to create a desk space. Pete's day job is graphic design – wedding invites, brochures, logos, that sort of thing. It wasn't exactly his dream to design bathroom catalogues, but I guess he gets to use some of his art skills and the company have been pretty accommodating about this whole thing, letting him try out remote working. He'll need to go back to the city every so often but, once we've got the internet connection sorted, he'll be all set up. Pete's hoping that we might be able to stay here long term, longer than my maternity leave. He thinks we'll fall in love with the mountains and want to stay our here; he thinks I'll want to leave my job when the baby comes and do something less stressful. I lie in bed while Pete's working and I can't help thinking about my office. What will they be doing right now? It's a Tuesday and it's still early, but Kim will be in already. She'll have been to her morning spin class and now she'll be striding about the place, spritzing her plants with water from an old hairspray canister, deciding on the day's case-loads, dropping piles of folders onto people's desks. I work for the Department of Housing, heading up emergency applications. Please state your reason for leaving your previous residence, the emergency form asks. And then it allows one line for a response. One line. Those lines are masterworks of pith; messy, woeful, intergenerational dramas condensed into a few words in tiny handwriting. 'Husband broke my collar bone now can't work.' 'Boyfriend tried to drown my son in bath hes a drunk got to get away or he kill us.' 'Neighbour attacked my son with fighting dog and says Abos spread disease.' We adopt a kind of gallows humour in the office. 'This one doesn't like the fungus in his flat,' someone will call across the room, 'fancies a stay at the Shangri-bloody-la.' 'Never mind that,' someone will call back in response, 'this one says her neighbours vacuum at "disturbing times" in the night. I wish my neighbours would vac the place anytime of the day or night.' I suppose me and Pete have done an emergency flit of a kind: what would I state as my one-line reason for leaving previous residence?

Insufficient income to rent habitable accommodation in the city, with a baby on the way…

Morbid fear of developing cutis symptoms due to environmental factors in current locale…

Obsessive recording and blogging of public-health risks in the city causing risk to my own livelihood and sanity…

My mother's dead eyes…

Everyone told us it was the right thing to do, to get out here while we had the chance. In fact, Kim practically pushed me out of the door. 'You get on out there, love,' she said. 'Sounds picturesque. Really it does. Beautiful place to spend your Mat Leave. HR will approve it starting early, 'course they will. You've seen the new disaster plan – they don't want a heavily-pregnant liability around the place!' I know the real reason she wanted me gone. A couple of months before, she'd taken me into The Black Hole, the tiny, windowless office we save for client interviews and disciplinaries.

'Babe,' she said. 'You know I'm your biggest fan.'

Kimmy recruited me fresh from college. She'd taken a chance on me, treated me as a sort of protégé: another sharp kid from the estates who wasn't part of the Old Boys' network. But Kim's no idiot: she'd spotted how keen I was to escape St Paul's, she knew that, if she recruited me, I'd be so grateful for the break that I'd graft like a navvy and pledge her my undying allegiance.

'Alice, you know I'd fight for you if it came to it. But I don't want it to come to that. That's why I'm giving you a heads-up. People are talking about you. Saying you're recording things, taking notes on cases. Personal notes.'

She kept her voice casual, paused here, blew her fringe off her face. She was giving me a chance to respond, to deny it. I said nothing.

'They're saying you're into some conspiracy stuff. Cutis related. They're *even* saying you're posting this stuff online.'

She pauses again. I keep my own counsel.

'Now, babe, I don't need to tell you that client confidentiality is a serious principle of this job, and that if HR got even a whiff of anything being put into the public domain relating to our clients– '

That does is: that pushes me over the edge.

'I'm not identifying anyone! And actually, what if confidentiality is putting our clients at risk? What if everyone is keeping quiet about something that's disproportionately going to affect our clients? Kill them even? What if they're leaving people untreated, leaving them with no proper care, leaving them to seal over, because they're not worth treating?'

Kimmy stutters her head back on her shoulders; she makes her eyes real wide, in an OTT oh-no-you-didn't gesture.

'Now, I'm going to pretend I didn't hear any of that. Because, just for a moment, Alice, that sounded like someone far less clever than you speaking. Someone, in fact, who was a fucking moron.' She leans back, eyeballing me. 'Ok. This is what we're doing. I'm telling people that you're not well. Pregnancy hormones, blah blah, death of your mother, blah blah. Everyone's going to get to hear that. You, meanwhile, are going to see Occupational Health, yeah, and you're requesting a session with the counsellor. Workplace stress, right? Grief counselling? And if any of this comes back to bite you on the fucking arse, you've got a paper trail of your derangement. Are you hearing me, Alice?'

I nod.

'Absolutely no more posting. And you fucking did this at work, Alice, where someone could see you? That someone being Phil? Phil, who applied for your promotion and would just love to see you hung out to dry? You need to sharpen up, you bloody goose.'

She stands up: this meeting is over. 'What have I always told you, Alice? You can't clear things from the bottom up. We need to get to the top and flush the crap back down the system.' She swoops in close to me. 'Keep your notes, but keep them safe at home, until we can do something here.'

* * *

I was careful at work after that, but I carried on with my records. I moved the blog, but I kept on posting. I needed to keep recording everything, to show people what was going on. Because people were already moving on, already forgetting about it. After that first headline, the story of the man at the dump, people had shared things online for a while. Reports from different parts of the world, strange photographs, rumours, all of it spread in a rash on people's media feeds and through forums. None of the big outlets were reporting it at first, so I kept on digging for info and I was already taking precautions, wearing my mask when the smogs were worst, watching what I ate. The stories people were sharing all featured unusual skin growths or aberrant scarring. And it wasn't just affecting mouths and noses: in some of the more lurid accounts, eyelids were knitting together, ears were closing up, genitals were folded back into sealed pudenda. Blurry photographs appeared, with the ambiguous lighting of ghost-hunter pictures, purporting to show the strange outgrowths of skin. One account described a man in California whose rectum had sealed over: he'd supposedly died from fecal vomiting, choking on his own shit. I'm not sure people believed that one, not literally, but there was a kind of grim, mythic logic to it, so we circulated the story anyway. Disgusted and compelled, we were all clicking 'share' as we ate chow mein or rode the tram to work.

The first official responses came when the post-mortem on the dead-dump-man was leaked to the press. The report described unusual skin adhesions across the man's mouth and nostrils, and the cause of death was determined to be asphyxiation. Journalists started unearthing other unusual deaths over the last couple of years, and there were plenty. There were suggestions of medical negligence, of a State-wide cover-up, of a global conspiracy. The newspapers caught up with the forums and started going wild then: was this a new pandemic, were all of us going to be choked in our beds by our own skin?

But this is what I still don't get: when real evidence began to emerge, people seemed less terrified. After that initial panic, interest began to just die down. And, after a while, most people just got back to normal. The reports named the new condition, *Cutis Sigillatis*, or the 'skin-sealing syndrome'. The Health Department published statistics on what it described as a small number of 'cutis-related deaths.' The condition was characterised by an overgrowth of the superficial epidermis, easily treated with surgery but causing serious complications if left untreated. The government called for calm: worldwide figures and patterns of emergence suggested rare, localised, abnormal skin behaviour. Surgeons in New York had already developed an effective perforation method to treat the condition: the excess skin growth was now known to be very thin and a few surgical perforations could be enough to undermine the new structure. Local cauterisation completed the procedure. There was no evidence that cutis was a communicable disease, incidences across the global population were low and were concentrated in densely populated urban areas and more remote areas with high atmospheric pollution. 'Think of it as a skin cancer,' a TV doctor pronounced breezily: 'stay vigilant and seek advice from your health-care provider if you notice anything unusual.' So, for most people, it became just one more thing among many to briefly worry about and then forget: the fires were getting worse and worse, the heat events more frequent, the rural-poor, indigenous folk, and migrants were being carted into camps every time it got too hot, there were Biblical floods on the other side of the world, our food was carcinogenic, our plastics were carcinogenic, the smogs were carcinogenic. Sometimes ash would float down through the haze, right in the middle of the city, blown in from hundreds of miles away. God knows what we were breathing. Add to that list: people's skin was going crazy in our toxic environment.

No one knew exactly what was causing it, of course. Studies were investigating all sorts of possibilities: BPA ingestion from plastics ('Is your baby's bottle poisoning her?'); triclosin absorption from cosmetics and detergents

('Is keeping clean poisoning our bodies?'); inhalation of $PM_{2.5}$ in smog-saturated and polluted cities ('Are greener cars choking us?'). For those with expensive tastes, protected food guaranteed an indoor-reared product, with minimal exposure to atmospheric pollution and chemical treatment. Those who could afford to bought the special food, bought their face masks for high-pollution days, bought their private insurance for high-spec surgery. Charity campaigns raised money for expert teams to be deployed in crisis areas, for street-children in global cities to get plastic surgery. In our city, the panic quickly died down. Small, emergency surgeries opened within bigger medical practices, and only poor people ever seemed to die from cutis – poor people far away, or poor people at home who didn't take care of themselves. The expert reports were clear: if you stayed vigilant, if you gave your five dollars to a medical charity and looked after yourself, you had nothing to worry about. Only the feckless and the faraway had anything to fear.

I could see what was really happening, the stuff that wasn't being reported. Something seemed to crop up at work almost every day, one way or another. An emergency housing request for a man who'd lost his job after a bodged cutis-correction to his eyes had left him partially sighted. A family who wanted to be re-housed because a child in their high-rise had 'the skin-sealing disease' and they were worried they'd contract it. An elderly woman who wanted to move because an emergency surgery had opened on her road and she was surrounded by queues of 'rude kids', and 'Abos' with 'screaming babies'. Her skin was itching and she was sure she was going to catch it from 'the dross on the road'. The worst case I came across was a man who was on our waiting list for sheltered accommodation. He'd been found dead in his bed, excrement smeared up his back, his mouth completely sealed over. I was one of the team who went to inspect his flat: the bedroom walls were covered with pornography, except the wall above his bed, on which he'd written in marker pen, I hate this place, I hate this place, I hate this place. His wife's ashes were stored in an urn on the kitchen counter. We couldn't locate any living next of kin. I went to his funeral, along with two colleagues from Welfare. That made three of us at the crematorium, all of us dressed in grey suits on a blisteringly hot day. Cause of death was officially recorded as starvation, not cutis. Nothing official to record this as a cutis-related death of any kind. He was a known alcoholic, awaiting assessment for schizophrenia, with a long history of self-neglect. No one knew how long he'd stayed alone inside his flat, alive, with his mouth sealed up. Those who didn't have the nous or the desire to seek help were being sealed up alive, and no one gave a damn or even recorded it.

So I started my own reports. I noted down cases whenever I encountered them, and not just of housing applicants – I began making records of the anecdotal reports I was hearing about the immigration detention centres, too. Eaglewood fell within my catchment, and I'd sometimes meet clients who'd been detained there, moving them into emergency accommodation if they'd been granted temporary visas. They're awful places, the detention centres, worse than prisons, because of the number of children; because of how hopeful some of the people still are, how sure they are that the way they're being treated must be due to some mistake, that something must change, now that they've made it all the way here. One girl in particular got to me: I drove her to a shelter and she sat in silence most of the way. She was stiff, walked and seated herself as though she'd been injured somewhere deep inside. I didn't want to pry about where she'd come from and what might have happened to her, but I wanted to make sure nothing had happened here, at the centre. They're privately run, the centres, and, since the new laws, no one can whistle-blow. The State does an annual inspection, which involves the men in uniforms acting real nice and the detainees staying real quiet, eyeing the guards, knowing they'll be left alone with them as soon as the suits leave. There have been scandals, of course. Up north, one centre was slammed by the inspectors: high rates of suicide, accusations from the detainees of rampant sexual abuse. The contract was given to another provider, all the staff were sacked – and then re-hired by the new company.

It's a deterrent against immigration, I've heard people say, knowing that our guards can fuck you up with total immunity, knowing they're sometimes as dangerous as the people you're trying to escape. 'No one hurt you, did they?' I asked that girl. 'I mean here, at the centre?' She bit her bottom lip until it paled, and she didn't answer my question. 'You can tell me,' I said. 'I'm nothing to do with the centre. I don't work for them.' She looked at me then, her eyes slow and sad, and she told me that no one had hurt her and that she was thinking about the family who had been kept in the room next to her. They had come from the same place as her, they'd travelled together, and the family had been refused temporary asylum; they weren't even given the year that she'd been granted. They were being deported next week. And, a few days ago, the father had developed the skin disease, she said. His right ear had filled with doughy flesh. She mimed the skin poofing-up around his ear. It wasn't life-threatening, the guards had told him, so he could access treatment back in his own country. The man hadn't even asked for treatment, she said, but there would be nothing for him at home where the war raged on, and now he could barely hear. She put her forehead against my passenger-seat window and she cried, soundlessly.

Thank Christ, I thought, thank Christ this girl and the family hadn't all come by sea. They'd be there still, on those island prisons we've made, our deadly castles marooned in the ocean beyond the reach of the law. No one inspects them: state of exception, we're told; the government is dealing with an unprecedented crisis in *illegal maritime arrivals*, we're told, which makes it like a war. People don't get off of those islands. Not even the children. We all know what's happening out there: cruelty will thrive on a lawless rock-face in the middle of the sea and I can guarantee that no one imprisoned there is getting treatment for anything, let alone cutis, which is costly to mend. Every so often a body washes up on the coast, too badly burned to determine cause of death. We're outsourcing our State brutality now.

And there are plenty of other places where cutis isn't being recorded properly, I'm sure of it. I don't get to see the Internal Displacement Camps much – they're mostly outside our State. But I did once 'buddy-up' with a colleague from the next territory, to inspect one of theirs. The camps are given idyllic names, some of them so euphoric they're poised between euphemism and straight-up sarcasm: 'Home Elizabeth', 'Rose Place', 'Hope Springs'. The one I inspected was called 'Kookaburra Grove': a new facility at the edge of a city, designed to house people displaced by heat events. Hypothetically, these camps are meant to house anyone who is at risk from fires or area dehydration. In practice, they're for folks evacuated from public housing, lots of poor rural folk, lots of indigenous folk, all removed from vulnerable areas in the bush.

I'm not sure what I was expecting the camp to look like, but I found myself surprised by it. I guess I must have been thinking the whole affair would look more transitory, and more shambolic: perhaps I'd pictured people and their belongings chaotically crammed into makeshift shelters, supplies piled up, animals circling, children crying, rows of chemi-loos. The truth was far tidier and far more sinister: the camp was a dense grid of low, regular dwellings built from breeze-block. It looked less like the final day of a music festival and more like a scrupulously managed, large-scale battery farm. It was spotless. And very quiet.

'Where is everyone?' I asked. We were walking along 'Sylvania Boulevard' with a smartly-dressed woman, the vice-president of the company who ran the camp (*Call me Linda, girls*): the orange dust that powdered all the 'streets' was staining her pale suede pumps as we processed up and down the grid. A suspicious mind might deduce that Linda was not overused to walking around the place.

It was mid-morning and I'd only seen one person outside of the huts: an elderly man who'd cowered as we'd passed him. So I asked again: 'Where is everyone?'

'Well,' said the woman, 'the children will be in classes. We have two schools on site. And anyone of working age will be in their assigned work-place training or on voluntary work-place out in the city. We bus them out and back again each day.'

She licked her lips; the dust was sticking to her pale purple lip-gloss too.

'Right,' I said. 'And what about the elderly and the sick? What about anyone not of working age?'

'We have a social facility,' she said. 'We can see it if you'd like? It's on the west side of the camp. All the huts have cable: we find a lot of the elderly residents prefer to stay in their quarters and watch TV. We don't encourage socialising in the streets or in the home. We find that the noise can disturb other residents. So we ask all residents to confine social activity to the socially-zoned areas.'

'Like this?' I ask, pointing at a small, stark playground: one slide, one roundabout, one set of swings, all empty.

'Yes,' the woman says. 'We have one social zone per 200 residences, as per our contract. We even have several open-air social spaces, for indigenous residents who may wish to congregate in the outside.' She looks very smug about this. 'And we have a dry-rule: we have all sorts of shops, which I'll show you in a moment. But no one sells liquor. Due to the…' This is the only stumble in the script that she makes all day. 'Due to the, um, the special problems that this demographic sometimes have with alcohol. We think it's a safer environment for all without that particular temptation in the way.'

'But residents can drink in their own properties, right?' I ask. 'I mean, they're displaced people. They're not in prison, right?'

Linda laughs, breezily. 'Right. Although, all properties technically remain the property of HappyHome. And we find that they remain in better order when booze is removed from the equation.'

We walk for a while longer. I haven't seen a single piece of rubbish the whole time we've been here.

'It's so tidy,' I say. 'How is it so tidy with such a dense concentration of residents?'

'Our janitors are responsible for the upkeep of the site and for all matters of housekeeping.'

The janitor: a position half-way between a hall monitor and a chief of police. I meet these guys later on, and they'd taser you soon as see a piece of litter.

'But people are free to go?' I ask. 'People have freedom of movement within and from the camp? They could leave for the city anytime they wanted?'

'Of *course*,' Linda says. 'We do have a curfew, for the peace of mind of residents. Generally, we find that residents don't want to seek accommodation elsewhere, when they understand the situation and what a good deal they've got here. The State has provided them with housing here, so they won't be offered anything in the city. And of course, they'd have to pay back their relocation compensation if they were to leave. And why would you want to leave such a clean and orderly facility? If I'm honest with you, and I know you won't like this coming from the State side, Alice, but if I'm honest with you, these places are better equipped than most of the old public-housing these folk have left.'

'And what about re-introduction? How do you manage them back into their homes? When the risk of the heat event lessens?'

The woman blinks hard a couple of times. The grit is blowing up everywhere, into our eyes and our hair. 'Oh,' she says. 'That's never happened.'

I turn to my colleague, Melissa. 'What does she mean? People aren't meant to be here long-term, right? This is an interim measure?'

'That's right,' Melissa says, carefully. 'Vulnerable residents are housed here when local services need to be shut down because of the imminent risk from heat events. But, so far, the alert has stayed high in all of the areas we've evacuated. And just think about it from our point of view: it's not worth resuming all of the services, healthcare, schools, social care, just for a few months at a time. In practice, we're finding that some residents stay here for the longer term.'

At the end of the visit, Melissa is ecstatic. This is the best-run camp she's been to, she says; she's very happy to say that HappyHome are more than meeting their contractual requirements. She'd go so far as to say the camp is exemplary. 'If your State is thinking about going down this route,' she says to me, making a big show of it, 'you should definitely come back to consult with HappyHome as a preferred provider.' Linda from HappyHome preens.

'I'd like to see the medical records for the camp,' I say.

My colleague looks embarrassed. 'That's not part of the inspection,' she says.

'Yes it is,' I say. 'I've got the paperwork. It's the State's responsibility to make sure adequate educational, medical and care provisions are in place. And it's my job, as out-of-State buddy, to ensure that the regulations for the inspection are followed.'

Linda looks unperturbed. 'Of course,' she says. 'I thought I'd given you that information when I showed you the surgeries and schools, and I gave you the figures on medical staff? What more would you like to see, Ms Ford?'

I want to see cutis diagnosis and treatment rates; I want to see morbidity and mortality rates, though I hide it a little, wrap it up in lots of other requests.

'Well, as you'll be aware, we have a duty of confidentiality to our residents. We can't make any individual records available. You'll need to go through the surgeries to get those figures. You'll need to apply for them, like you would in the city.'

'But you keep figures on morbidity and mortality rates, like the Department of Health would?'

'Our surgeries hold those figures,' Linda says.

'So how are you monitoring public health?' I say. 'Given that your medical surgeries are private practices?'

'Our medical teams report into the Department of Health, just like any other private surgery in the city.'

'But there's a difference here,' I say. 'You're paying these fellas. It's in their interest to minimise treatment costs for you, right?'

Linda smiles. 'I'm sorry, ladies, you've been here for six hours, and I really do need to draw our meeting to a close. I've provided everything that's required as part of our inspection, and I'm delighted that you find our little place exemplary.'

Melissa sends out a complaint about me: apparently I was bullish and obstructive, and their State doesn't want me to 'buddy-up' for any future inspections. I go ahead and request the figures from the camp's surgeries anyway. And what I find is an unusually high mortality rate for young people living at the camp. And not one single cause of death recorded as cutis. In fact, no records at all of any cutis diagnoses or surgical interventions. The surgery is costly: they're leaving it untreated and burying it without a trace, they have to be.

I added all this to my files, which were growing more and more extensive. And then, of course, there was my mother. My mother who died of a heart attack, my mother who, according to official medical records, absolutely did not die of cutis. So you see, with all this going on, I had to carry on recording things, even after Kimmy's warning. I had to record the signs, hidden but everywhere, of what was really going on.

* * *

It's late afternoon by the time Pete's finished his work and we're ready to set off down the road in search of the neighbours. We walk side by side and we swing our arms. Pete seems happy, carefree almost.

'How was work?' I ask.

'Not too shabby,' says Pete. 'Just finishing up a job. Jet-ski brochure.'

'Yeah?' I say.

'Look at this,' he says, turning towards the valley and the mountains. 'No smog out here. Clean as a whistle. Smell that air!'

I breathe in through my nose. It smells cleaner than the city, for sure. It's a complex mix, there are tones in there: the hot acacia hits you first, green and waxy, but then there's something sharper, a bit like petrol, and after-notes of charcoal ash. Things smell different to me now, stronger and more distinct. Before we left the city, I'd stopped going out on weekends when there was smog. I could smell the pollution hours before it descended: I could distinguish all the different acrid layers that make up its piss-yellow haze. It made me dizzy and nauseated. Pete says it's the pregnancy, says it can make you hyper-alert to scents and tastes. Says his mother could smell bacon when it was being cooked three streets away when she was pregnant with his youngest brother. I keep quiet about the petrol smell and let Pete enjoy all his outdoor gasping.

When we reach the neighbour's house, it's just as it was yesterday: deserted except for the fat cat lying out on the front porch in the sun, like the king of his own prairie. Pete walks up the path and I follow. As we get closer, I see that above the cat there's a dense canopy of spider webs. Some of them are worked over so thickly that they've got the fluffy look of raw cotton. I can see the fat, black, carnivorous centres of several of them. 'It's the spit of our house, hey bub? Its little twin.' Pete crouches down and coos at the cat. The cat regards him with deep contempt. Pete reaches out his hand. In the sunlight, I can see that the cat's long, white fur is full of dust and pollen, and god knows what else, and that if Pete touches it he'll feel its horrible, hard knots of mange and his fingers will come back coated in filth. 'Don't,' I say, though I needn't have. The cat has made its fur even bigger, sinking its head back between its shoulders, hissing at Pete. It slinks off the porch.

'Who's there?' a voice shouts from inside the house.

Pete stands up, grins at the doorway. The door's open, but there's a black mosquito net strung across it and it's too dark inside to make anything out.

'Watch yourself,' I say to Pete, pointing up at the dense, white webs above the doorway. No one can have been out here for months. I stand well back on the path and Pete nods, staying off the porch.

'G'day!' he calls. 'We're your new neighbours. Just moved in up the road. Thought we'd say hello!' Pete turns to me. 'Shit,' he says. 'Should've brought something. Beers? Flowers?'

'Clear-off,' the voice shouts. 'We're not going anywhere.' The shout is an elderly man's: it sounds raw, as though the sound is being ripped from his throat. At the ends of his sentences the sound splits in unpredictable ways; his voice is breaking again in a reverse adolescence. 'Bugger right off.'

Pete laughs, turns to me with a check-this-bloke-out expression. 'Sir,' he says, 'you've misunderstood me. We're just here to introduce ourselves. We've moved in, further up the street. We're living up at Mountain View, so we're neighbours.'

The man appears to be sidling up to the edge of the door, to get a better look at us. I can see the dark outline of his shoulder, and half his face is almost visible, blurred behind the black screen.

'A'right,' Pete says. 'My name's Pete and this is Alice. As you can see, we're expecting.' Pete always says this so proudly. He even leans back a little on his heels, as though he's the one who's carrying and having to recalibrate his centre of gravity. There's no reply from the man and he's moved his face back out of the doorframe. Then there's a shuffling sound, which seems to come from further inside the house; it's a bit like someone clearing their throat, or another exhausted attempt to speak.

'Clear-off,' the man cries again, though his voice sounds

less convincingly hostile. 'You don't want to be hanging around here. Get out of it.'

'Mate,' says Pete, taking a step forward. 'We really don't mean any trouble. It's just we haven't got anything set up yet, in our new place, and, as I said, Alice here is expecting. Do you have a phone-line down here? We might need to use it, if there was an emergency.'

'Knew you'd want something,' the man says and it sounds as though he spits. 'You're not coming in here. No one's coming in here,' he says. 'Always trying to get us to leave, bloody sticky-beaks, telling us it's not safe out here, and then coming in here and making her sick.'

'Who's sick?' I call out. I step forward and it's then that I notice the smell. It's subtle, but there's something else there alongside the grass and the warm eucalypt. The smell is too interesting to be disgusting, at first. It's not a common smell. It's sharp and sweet, a little bit like vinegar, but more earthy. More intimate. There's a metallic tang to it too. I finally place it: it's a smell from back at school, from the summer when everyone got their ears pierced. We had to turn the little gold studs in our lobes every day, to stop them crusting over. We'd do each others' in the playground at break time. When you broke the crust, something wet would leak out onto your fingers. And it was that smell in the air, the smell of tiny scabs, trying to heal and being broken. A warm smell of skin and pus.

'Rack off,' the man shouts again. 'I mean it. You don't want to hang around here. Get off my land.'

'Listen, mate,' Pete's still trying, ever hopeful. 'We've got off on the wrong foot. We're just here to say hello.'

'Let's go,' I say to Pete. The smell is unnerving me. Why would a man's house smell of weeping earlobes?

'I've got a gun,' the man shouts, and to demonstrate his point he waves something long and thin behind the netting.

'Chri'sake,' Pete shouts, 'we're only being friendly.' Pete has moved his body in front of mine and is jostling me back down the path. 'Bloody mentalist,' he says to me. 'That's not a gun, it's the handle of a tennis racket or something.'

'Clear-off,' the man carries on shouting. 'Fucking wogs. That's right. Get off my land. Bloody sticky-beaks.' He carries on shouting until his voice warbles off, hoarse and painful.

It's late and once again I can't sleep. I'm listening to Pete breathing heavily beside me and I'm listening to the unfamiliar animal noises outside and I'm thinking about the man down the road and why we ever came out here. The whole of the last year now feels like a horrible, mad blur: I was so preoccupied with my glimpses of cutis, with posting them on my blog, with all of the horrible shit involved in sorting out Mum's affairs (having to tell strangers over the phone – strangers at the utility companies, strangers

73

at banks, strangers at the local housing board – over and over again that my mother had died: 'Oh we're so sorry to hear that,' appropriate pause, 'do you have a certificate you could send?'; there was always a piece of paper to reproduce, to photocopy again and again to prove that she no longer existed, until all that was left of grief was the thin, papery feeling as I posted one more proof of death), I was so preoccupied that I failed to deal with this enormous problem growing inside me.

When I found out I was pregnant, I booked a termination consultation. And I missed it. I booked it again. And I missed it again. I suppose I never really believed in it, my pregnancy: even when the test said positive – the first one, when I soaked the stick in pee and stared at it for an age, waiting for it to change again, for the little line to shrink back again, and then the second and the third and finally the doctor's test – even then I still couldn't believe it. I couldn't believe that my body would carry this thing to term. I couldn't believe that in the middle of all of the chaos and suffering, something could thrive and grow. So I ignored it, mostly. Perhaps I was daring my body in some strange and reckless way: go on, just see if you can make something, just see if you can make something new and good in the midst of all this.

Pete called me when I was a few months gone, said he knew, said his mum had seen me in the street and told him I looked 'puffy', and why hadn't I bloody told him myself, and was it his, and he didn't care if it was or it wasn't, he loved me, he'd always loved me, we should be together, we should give ourselves another chance, a proper chance.

We met in a café in the city centre one night after work. I didn't think I looked pregnant: my stomach was softer but not yet swollen. My face was softer too, I guess, a new puffiness beginning to be detectable. I'd seen Pete's mum, Eleni, in the street, when I was checking for post at Mum's flat, and I thought I'd deflected her. 'Alice,' she'd said. 'You look unwell. Have you been crying? Come inside.' 'I'm fine,' I said. She'd eyed me suspiciously: 'Your face is swollen, my love. You've been crying? Come and have dinner with us. The boys are all out.' I'd refused. Did my face really look that different? Or was it some weird, grandmotherly intuition? Whatever it was, it had brought me here now, to sit with Pete while he made a case for us trying to be together again.

'We've given it a go already,' I said to him. 'We were happy, for a bit, and then we were both more unhappy than we've ever been. Remember?'

'That was different,' he said. 'That was years ago. We were still kids really, Ali, both of us.'

We were not kids; not exactly. And I resented the implication that we were both equally at fault, that our break-up was the result of youth and nothing else, nothing

Pete had done. But what were my other choices, really? A late-term abortion? Bringing a child up on my own in a bedsit? Everyone who might help me was gone: since my mother's death, I'd let friendships lapse, burying myself in my records ever deeper. At least Pete was still there, loveable Pete and his enormous family, ready to take me in. And when he suggested we move out here, try to take care of ourselves and become a proper family, part of me wanted a rest. At least, part of me hoped I might remember how to rest.

So here we are, in the middle of nowhere. In the foothills of the mountains, where the eucalypt oil fills the sky and turns the earth blue. Where animals scream in the night and the neighbours threaten to kill us. Here we three are, waiting to be a family.

IV

'YOU'RE moaning, babe,' Pete's voice says in the darkness. 'And grinding your teeth. Wake up, Ali. It's just a nightmare.'

The dream has faded instantly to black – I can't remember a thing. But I can still feel the adrenaline. I'm breathless and my heart flutters. I'm covered in a filigree of sweat, which is cooling quickly. It makes me shiver. I feel a movement above my hip, sharp and painful: I put my hand down there, into the soft tissue, and I can feel a curve of bone that isn't my bone. A hard foreign body. Its head, I think, or its own hip. I draw my hand away.

My dreams are sometimes so vivid these days that it's hard to tell where they stop and waking begins. It's worse now the bump's gotten so big – it's lively at night, and even before we got out here I could only sleep in fitful snatches. In some of my dreams we're back at home, in my mother's flat, on St Paul's, at the edge of the city. And it's the only place left: the world is a crater and her maisonette is perched at the edge of it. Sometimes she saves me: she takes me down into a cellar that the flat never had, she digs it out with her bare hands, and she keeps me safe while everything rages outside. The cellar grows bigger and bigger, she digs more and more of it out, and then we're living in an enormous bulb, like an onion, something that will blossom when the spring returns, casting me and the baby out into the air as pollen. Sometimes I dream like this. Usually, though, the dreams are less hopeful. I'm with a group of people I know, back in the city, and the people are talking normally, a low patter of talk punctuated with polite laughter. Martha from HR might turn to me – it's a work meeting – and she'll ask me casually about whether I've completed the mentoring checklist for my new starter. As she speaks, something strange starts happening to Martha's face. The skin of her neck is rippling slightly; the movement is actually visible, a subtle subcutaneous wave. The skin of her throat seems to be filling up with something, straining, until suddenly it crests up over her chin, spilling across her mouth, and her words are eaten up as the skin rolls up and up, and then she's buried in a mini-avalanche of pudgy beige matter, her features disappeared into this solid fudge. Martha's face is morphed into a featureless slab of flesh, and the people around us just keep on talking. Sometimes I dream about the baby being born and disappearing immediately between

78

my thighs, swallowed up in folds and folds of my own skin, suffocated at birth. Walled-up forever inside me.

Often it's just my mother's face I see. I didn't touch it, in the hospital. I wanted to, but I was too afraid. In the dreams, my hand reaches out to touch her eyes and her skin roils up towards me, moving for a moment like silk on a breeze, then beginning to bury my arm.

Perhaps it's a good thing I can't remember last night's dream.

'I'm getting up,' Pete says. 'I'm going to head into town. I want to report that man.'

'What do you mean, report him?' Yesterday, as we walked back from the old man's place, Pete had tried to make light of it, joking about the threats, describing the old man as a rolling-pin assassin. But he kept coming back to it, all evening. I could see that the old man had bothered him. He must've been thinking about him all night.

'He seemed pretty sick,' Pete says. 'He was real skinny. It's off-colour, him being all on his own. That place is in a state.'

'There was a smell,' I say. 'Something not right.'

'That's it,' Pete says. 'Something's not right there.'

'So who are you going to report him to?' I ask.

'Well, there must be a Social Services office,' he says. 'He mentioned Social Services.'

'I wouldn't bank on it,' I say. 'Not a local one, at any rate.'

'Police station, then,' he says.

'Oh yeah?' I say, 'You going to report him for threatening us with a broom handle?'

'I'm going to report that he seems unwell,' he says. 'A possible danger to himself. I don't get it. Old people out here on their own. Where are his kids? Where are his nephews?'

'This would never happen in a Greek family,' I say, anticipating his next line.

'No!' he says. 'It wouldn't!'

'And what would your mother say to that?' I ask. 'She'd say, "You're a Slavic-Greek, Peter. No one is just one thing. Places are not just one place. It's com-pli-ca-ted."'

He gives me a look, a frown that turns quickly to tenderness. I think we're going to laugh together at my impression of Eleni, before I realise that he's not really looking at me: it's the bump he's looking at so tenderly.

'What do you think he meant, when he said *they made her sick*?' I try to sound casual as I ask this. I turn onto my back and wriggle around a bit on the mattress. There's no real way to get comfy. My stomach feels tight and itchy this morning. The stretched skin on my abdomen has gone dry and there's a new texture at the sides of the bump, where the skin is cleaving in a sort of raggedy, glinting pattern. It's like exposed elastin, or a sudden reveal of silverfish just below my surface. And there's a dark line through the centre of it all now, bisecting my stomach. I try not to look at it. I turn back to Pete. 'Do you think there's someone else in there with him?' I ask. 'Someone sick?'

'What, in the house with him?' Pete says. 'Oh, right, I see where this is going. You're going to tell me there's someone with cutis in there. He's an old, sick man, Alice. Sick in the usual way. You saw that porch. If there was ever a *her*, she's long gone. I'm off,' he says, and kisses my damp cheek.

When Pete's gone, I lie in bed for a while, watching the intermittent movements under the surface of my stomach. Sometimes I think I can make out the shape of a tiny fist, punching itself upwards and out. It makes me remember gruesome revenge tales about children baked in pies and all those gory nursery rhymes: four and twenty blackbirds fluttering to escape their crust. The floury skin of my belly is a pastry case as I drum my fingers against it, its live filling wriggling to get out.

I have to get up to retch, and then I wander into the little room that Pete's calling the 'nursery'. I haven't really paid much attention to the things in here. It's mostly stuff we've been given by Pete's family. There's an old crib, the one that Pete and his siblings all slept in. It's not picturesque. It's from the '90s and it's massive. The varnish on the light wood is peeling away in tea-coloured slews, like sunburnt skin. That must be dangerous. God knows what sort of chemicals were used to treat wood back then. The mattress is soiled and looks lumpy. We don't have any bedding yet. The only other furniture in here is a set of drawers. I open the top one, which is full of small sets of clothes, neatly folded. I didn't do any of this, Pete must have packed this all away, with unusual care. I glance down at my massive belly alongside the contents of the drawer, and it's such an alien scene that for a moment I feel as though I'm an intruder: I've broken into this house, I'm looking into someone else's drawers, I'm in someone else's body. I'm watching a film about a pregnant woman, close third-person. My real body is somewhere else, back in the city, hard and compact and entirely my own, watching all of this. A hand reaches out and touches the baby clothes. These are donations too. Pete's mother worried we hadn't thought about the details and tried to make up for my evident lack of enthusiasm about outfits and blankets and prams and pumps. The hands in front of me, the pregnant woman's hands, are unfolding a little yellow baby-grow. Pete's mum must have kept all these things for decades. There's a picture of a bunny on the front of the tiny garment, printed in some kind of thin, adhesive plastic. Where the material has been folded the print is cracking, and the colours have faded, so that the middle of the rabbit's face, up to and including its eyes, is a blur. The baby-grow looks like it has myxomatosis. I shove it back in the drawer. All of this stuff is bloody toxic. I can taste it, the plastic in the air, the carcinogens. The door slams shut as I leave the room. I'm not going near it again.

I try to eat breakfast, but nothing will stay down. I wish I could call her now, Eleni, Pete's mum. Pete is one of four, with innumerable cousins. Eleni is not one of those euphoric birth evangelists. She always makes childbirth sound like a deeply unpleasant but necessary procedure, a bit like a bad trip to the dentist or giving evidence in court. She makes casual pronouncements like, 'Of course, I couldn't sit down for a fortnight after Pete. Scissored to kingdom come. But John bought me a rubber ring and we got on just fine.' In the early stages, I didn't want to hear any of her dour advice. It was mortifying, the things she'd bring up after dinner. I didn't want to think about the precautions needed to guard against piles or protect my perineum, and I certainly didn't want everyone else thinking about them over milk pie. But, right now, hearing her voice, her grim, phlegmatic pronouncements, and, behind them, her unshakeable belief that whatever happens, you just get on with it – right now, I'd like to hear that. She'd tell me straight-off if this is normal, the sickness and the crawling sensation across my skin and the darts of electricity through my abdomen.

I drop an unfinished slice of protected bread and marmalade into the bin and try to think of ways to keep myself busy. I could re-organise some of our things in the kitchen cupboards: Pete has thrown everything in in a haphazard manner, so that the pans in one cupboard are surrounded by tea-lights, and a colander in another is filled with napkins and cutlery. I start to get everything out, so that I can produce sensible taxonomies. I arrange all the pans across the floor in families of use. Dishes are arranged in groups according to size. Cutlery is bunched together, and then subdivided into different clans, the spoons being the most populous. I sit down on the floor and begin to sort through some of the old earthenware I saved from Mum's flat. But, as I reach across to sort through the plates, something inside me pushes hard up into my ribs, causing a sharp stab of pain through my sternum. I grab at my stomach, breathless. I sit upright, very still, waiting to see if the pain will come again. It does, and this time I can see the movement, something angular momentarily protruding at the top of my stomach. I've seen the scan pictures. I know that I'm meant to imagine that this is a baby, that its adorable little foot or elbow is pushing against me. Everyone told me the scan would be the moment when it all made sense, when I would see it and fall in love with what was inside me. The midwife said I should start talking to the baby then, start trying to bond with it. She said that it could hear my voice already. So I watched carefully as the grainy body parts appeared on the screen at the hospital and the cold-handed woman pushed deep into my stomach with the probe in her relentless search for heart valves and lips and genitals. 'Look there,' she said, clacking her nails across the screen. 'No cleft palate.' And Pete beamed at my side, looking grateful and overwhelmed, given an award he didn't even know he'd been nominated for. He'd never heard of cleft palate, he told me afterwards. That's Pete all over: graced with the bliss that comes from ignorance of danger. That scan was it for him: he believed in it all, he could picture a beautiful, healthy baby. It never felt like that for me; the thing inside me was still impossible. I suppose I'd have to feel the wounds, put my hands right in the flesh. And in these moments, when I think about what's inside me, I still can't believe it: I can't believe those weird parts we saw on the screen will add up to a person. Right now, I see the palpitations in my stomach again and I imagine giving birth to a bundle of flesh with no shape; to something entirely sealed in, an oily mass of meat with fists and heels and a skull, without a single orifice. I feel a burning rush of nausea again and get up onto my feet.

I stand over the sink for a while, trying to focus on the concrete things around me. I suck up some water and I look out across the garden, towards the mountains. There's no rustling in the undergrowth today and I can see birds wheeling about, high above the valley, riding the thermals. Maybe Pete's right and all of this anxiety is just the hormones. Maybe I see danger everywhere because of an instinct to protect. Pete makes it sound as though it's a positive thing, as though all of my apocalyptic imaginings are a healthy maternal response that's just got a bit out of hand. He's always ready to see the best in a situation; and in me. I look out at the mountains and the blue-grey haze around them. It's not like the smog back in the city; there's nothing yellow or septic-looking about it. The softening of the mountain edges is just distance, and eucalypt oil on the air, and low, fine cloud. I breath out. The nausea has passed.

When he gets back from town, Pete looks distracted. He's bought some beers and he cracks open a bottle straight-off.

'How was it?' I ask.

'Not great, babe,' he says. 'Couldn't find anyone who gave a rat's arse about the old bloke.' He lifts the bottle towards his mouth and sucks off the soapy bubbles at the neck. 'It's weird. There's hardly anyone about.'

'What do you mean, weird?' I ask. 'It's a small town. It's not going to be like the city.'

Pete's not looking at me. He's not good at keeping things to himself. I can see he's struggling with something.

'Look, just tell me what's going on,' I say. 'I'm not going to get hysterical. Give me some credit.'

He looks up at me. His eyes flicker across my face and down to my belly, and I can see that he's making a quick calculation about my present levels of reasonableness. He's not convinced.

'It was nothing, really, babe,' he says. 'Some of the services were just… a bit dismissive.' He swigs his beer.

'Doesn't surprise me,' I say. 'There's hardly any funding out here. So who did you speak to?'

'Well, I went to the police station first, to ask where I should go to make a report. They had this old-fashioned bell on the counter, and when I finally spoke to the bloke behind the desk, he told me Social Services are… well, they've shut them down for the area. Everything's being centralised in the next district. So I went down to the doctors' surgery. Thinking the old coot had shouted about the district nurse, so maybe they knew about him. Christ, Ali, the doctors' was bedlam.'

'I know,' I say. 'I tried to tell you.'

Pete is drinking his beer quickly and he's still not looking at me. 'Were there any symptomatics?' I ask. 'When I was there, there was a little boy,' I say, and it feels good to talk about it, 'and he was covering his ears and just whining. I'm pretty sure it was cutis.'

Pete looks up at me. We look at one another for a long moment, for long enough that it feels like we're properly together again, and Pete's face is, in that moment, the same, round, gentle face of Anderson Avenue: the face of the beautiful boy next door, the boy who would climb into our garden at night to drink blackcurrant juice with me and Mum under a blanket, who would wait for me after school to show me an unusual rock he had found in the playground, who would sit at our kitchen table to do his homework when his own house was too noisy and full of shouting siblings. My mother loved Pete. He was the kind of kid who always had filthy clothes, and his fingers in his mouth, and a big graze he'd be picking at, constantly lifting its edges and reforming the wound. Mum would tut fondly at his filthy habits and she loved having him in the house. He would pick flowers for her and sit on our doorstep like a hopeful orphan. And she was always pink-faced and happy when she was chiding him. She saved things up for his frequent visits: food, and books I'd finished with, and all the affection that I didn't want.

He's not that boy anymore. Or, at least, he is for only a moment. He looks away from me. He tilts the beer back into his mouth. His jaw is stronger now and he's clenching his teeth so that there are pits in his cheeks. Pete has grown up into that mix of soft and hard that people find appealing in a man: his dark, soft skin, his bright, glittering eyes, alongside the strong chin and massive shoulders. The contrast is in his moods too. He's buoyant, a perennial optimist, but he has short, wild bursts of anger, and of recklessness. I've always been more steadily pessimistic, more consistently angled. A gangly child and a hard-featured woman. 'Sharp,' my mother used to say. 'You've got your father's sharpness.'

High cheekbones, a hawkish nose, vivid lips. The sort of face that made people think I was haughty, even as a child. The sort of face that gets you punished.

'So,' I ask again. 'What was it? What did you see? Were there symptomatics?'

'Ali,' Pete says, 'it was… horrible.'

I sit down next to him. 'Tell me,' I say. 'Tell me what they looked like.'

Pete knocks back the beer again. He's almost drained the bottle. 'I'm not sure you want to hear this, babe,' he says.

'I need to know what's going on,' I say. 'I'm not recording things, I'm not going to post anything out here, am I? You need to tell me.'

Pete looks at me again. He takes my hand and he stares at me and his eyes widen in that pleading, desperate way he sometimes has just before he comes. His mouth parts, and now I can see how frightened he really is, how much he wants to tell me. But then he glances down at my stomach. His jaw clenches again. He looks away for a few seconds, blinking hard, shuttering something away. When he looks back at me he's fastened his face back together, collected and resolute. He places my hand carefully on top of my bump and wipes the back of his across his mouth.

'It must just be the systems here,' he says. 'They're less well equipped than the city, that's all.'

'What did you see?' I ask. 'What were people's symptoms?'

'Look, it's nothing we haven't heard about before. It just shook me up, seeing people. They're all getting treatment, they'll be ok. Let's just try to forget everything about today and have a nice, relaxing evening.'

'What was it?' I ask again. I'm trying to keep my breath steady and my voice level, but I can hear my own words, weirdly sticky, catching in my throat. Excess mucus production. Another joy of pregnancy. I swallow, and it's sour and thick. 'Where were the symptoms? Was it people's ears, like that boy? Or mouths? Or eyes? What did you bloody see?'

'I knew it,' he says, 'I knew I shouldn't have said anything. Of course you'd go over the top.' He gets up, pushes his chair away from the table. 'Poor buggers don't need you with your sticky-beak in their symptoms, recording everything in your morbid little files. And who's it good for, anyway, Alice, any of this? You're just getting yourself worked up, and me now as well. And stress is bad for the baby. Chri'sake.'

He opens the door to the verandah and blunders out. He's pacing about outside, muttering under his breath. A familiar panic is starting to rise up my throat. I rest my hand on my collarbone. I can feel my pulse flickering in my throat through my fingertips. I place my thumb on my windpipe, pressing gently. There are ridges in the cartilage here, hard little circles. They're moving up and down together as I keep on swallowing, trying to get rid of the phlegm. The movement's like a brown snake's when it's taken on something too big for it. I keep on: I've got to clear my throat, my breathing already feels restricted. Another thing no one tells you about pregnancy: that your baby will take your space to breathe, growing upwards, contracting your lungs. At six months I had to stop half-way up staircases. I stopped gasping after a couple of weeks, got used to my newly compressed lungs. But now this, this new attempt to stop me breathing, with mucus and panic. I grip my windpipe, rub my fingers up and down, up and down. It's nubbed, the trachea; brittle but flexible. My mind flickers back to those images we saw on the screen, of the strange, bony thing curled up in my pelvis. Its little spine, its own ridged columns already forming inside me, an echo of my own. We saw a dead lamb once, Pete and me. We were on a weekend hiking trip and it was curled at the edge of a ranch. It had come too soon, the lamb, and its bones weren't properly formed. Something had eaten it out from the middle, so that it was wearing its skin like a savaged shawl: head and legs still intact, but the centre entirely gone. You could see its tiny spinal-column, lain out like a row of pearls. The bone was translucent, only half-hardened, glistening in the sun. It had come too early. I run to the sink, and I cough and I cough and I spit into the bowl until my throat is raw and clear.

* * *

Pete comes back inside after a while. He's drunk. He might even be a bit stoned. It's difficult to tell with Pete – sometimes, when his mood is high, he's so blithe he seems stoned anyway. He holds my hand and he covers it in kisses. He looks happy and tearful and he tells me that he loves me, and he loves the baby, and that we're all safe. He says he's sorry that he got worked up, that he knows he should be more understanding. I kiss him back and try to shrink my anger, to swallow it down with all the mucus and the bile. But whenever I try to do that, whenever I try to make my anger disappear, it just gets harder and more compact, like sedimentary rock, and then I'm left with this hard stone in my chest. I give up on asking what he saw at the doctors'.

'Babe,' he says. 'The good thing about the trip into town was that I bumped into Paulie.'

'Paulie?'

'Paulie. Your remember. Nice bloke from the pub in town. We got to talking. He's got a girlfriend and a kid, you know. I invited them over for a beer. Thought it'd be nice for you to meet someone else with a baby out here.'

'Right,' I say.

'So they're coming over tonight. Just for a quick pop in. I've got in loads of tinnies.'

He moves away from me and starts getting busy in the kitchen now, pouring unprotected crisps into bowls, then licking the yellow dust off his fingers. He turns and gives me a killer grin: 'Our first guests, Ali. Look at this. Me and you, entertaining. Like a proper little family.'

'When?' I say. 'When are they coming over?'

''Bout now,' he says.

Pete's happy when there's a bang on the door a little while later. Turns to me with a look that says: 'Here I go! Answering *our* front door!' I've been watching him for any signs that he's still upset. I know he was scared by what he saw in town, I saw it in his face. But as he tidied up the living-room, set out the camping chairs, opened another beer, there was no sign of any fear left. He started whistling and put some music on. It's gone: the anxiety has passed through him quick as clouds across a blue, wind-blown sky.

When Pete opens the door, Paulie's standing on the step.

'A'right,' Paulie says. He's wearing a cap and he pushes it further back on his head. Then he puts out a hand. And he instantly regrets it, he regrets putting out his hand. He's uncertain: I can see it in the tiny waver in the hand that he holds out. He's just a nervous kid after all, and I regret acting hostile back in the bar.

Pete grabs Paulie's hand and turns the greeting into a half-hug. 'Alright, mate,' he says. 'Good to see you. Come on in.'

Paulie steps across the threshold, takes his cap off. His coney-coloured hair is damp and flat against his head. 'Here she is,' he says, thumbing over his shoulder. 'My quadroon and our little half-breed.' Nope, I was right the first time: he's a malicious little boy, chock-full of spite.

'Stop being a bloody pig,' the woman says. 'Paulie likes to act up, don't you, babe? Likes to get up people's noses.' She steps inside and swats her free arm against his backside. A small child is propped-up in her other arm and he holds clumps of her long, dark hair in both of his fists. His little mouth hangs open, as he stares at me and then at Pete. His cheeks are streaked with old tears. 'I'm Mara,' the woman says, 'Nice place you've got here.' She smiles, a wide and slightly goofy grin. Her face is broad, her jawbone half a hexagon. And her skin is super radiant: the colour of bronze, burnished with perspiration, a dark red blush at the apples of her cheeks. She looks so healthy, her skin seems almost metallurgic. And she looks happy. Maternal glow, I guess – or else the air really is clear out here.

'Good to meet you, Mara,' Pete says. 'And who's this little fella?' Pete swoops in real close, trying to take the child's hand. The baby just stares at Pete, eyes brimming with fury. His tiny hand clenches harder and then he flails out at Pete's face. He strikes Pete on the mouth and immediately starts to wail.

'Oh, lord, I'm sorry,' says Mara. 'He's called Iluka, Luke for short.' The child has buried his face in Mara's neck now and his back is palpitating.

Paulie is cough-laughing. 'Killer right hook my little man's got there.'

'What can I say,' Pete says. 'I've got a knack with the little ones. Bodes well, right? Sit down, won't you? Have a seat on the sofa, Mara, I'll fix us some drinks.'

Mara settles into the corner of our couch with the child, and I take the seat next to her while Pete clatters around in the kitchen behind us.

'You must be Alice,' she says, though she's only half-looking at me. She's preoccupied with the wriggling child in her arms. She brings her lips down to his face and murmurs, trying to soothe him.

'That's right,' I say. Paulie is leaning back in one of our camp chairs. Looks like he's ready to test it to breaking point. 'Sorry about the seating,' I say, 'We're still getting set up.'

Paulie shrugs his shoulders in an I-don't-give-a-shit-about-your-domestic-arrangements kind of a way, but he stops bracing back in the chair. 'Looks alright to me,' he says. 'If you need stuff, let us know. There used to be a Salvo Army in town. Closed down now. I've got mates who do removals over in the next territory, always got stuff they want to unload.'

'Ta,' I say. 'Pete has grand plans to build bookshelves. We'll see if that ever happens.'

'Righto,' Paulie says.

'So, you must be pretty far along?' Mara says. The baby's disappeared under her top; I guess he's feeding now.

'Thirty-six weeks,' I say. I shift slightly, trying to get comfy. I watch Iluka's little feet twitching with pleasure, his grubby baby socks and the soft, buttery skin of his chubby calves above them. Impossible to think that my bump, this thing inside me, is going to be as real and alive as the wriggling thing in Mara's arms.

'This your first?' Mara asks.

'Yep.'

'Oh, I remember that feeling,' she says. I'm expecting her to elaborate. She doesn't.

Pete's cursing in the kitchen. 'Everyone alright with warm beer?' he shouts through. 'Fridge is on the bleedin' blink.'

'It'll do,' Paulie says.

'Yeah, I'm not fussed,' Mara says.

'I'll have that lemonade, babe,' I call through.

Pete fusses about for a bit, bringing through the drinks and little bowls of snacks. Eventually he clinks with everyone and then eases himself into a camp chair.

'So, how old's Iluka?' he asks.

'Nearly ten months,' Mara says, but she's only half with us. The baby has fallen asleep on her breast and we all watch as she draws him into the nook of her arm, rocking him gently. There's watery milk swimming around his lips. Mara moves her lips across the top of his head, whispering against his soft skull. I've always found it kind of obscene, this intimacy between mothers and their babies: she's lost in the baby and her lips rustle against his skin. Is she blissed out, I wonder, or is she speaking a secret spell of protection? Keep him safe, Almighty Lord, God of our Dreaming, help me keep my baby safe from harm. The thing is, it doesn't matter how hard you pray, or what you whisper. I've read about the contamination of breast milk: they've found paint stripper and DDT and flame retardant in there. She could be poisoning him right now. We're all bringing our babies into harm, one way or another.

'Well, he's growing up strong, from what I can tell,' Pete says.

'That boy's going to be strong as an ox,' Paulie says, swigging back his beer. 'How you finding it up here?' he says, looking across at me. 'Quiet enough for you?'

'Oh, it's a beaut,' Pete says. 'Just what we were after, isn't it, Alice? A break from all that smog and stress in the city. Great place to start a family.'

'You reckon?' Paulie says.

'There used to be a big old camp up here,' Mara says, looking up from the child, 'just the other side of the street. You seen the clearing in the jarrah? Just there. It's traditional land, you know. When I was young there were still a few folk left up here, some of them living in cars. I'd come up sometimes to visit,' she says. 'Some of my mother's folks were here.'

'Oh yeah?' says Pete.

'Yeah,' says Paulie, brusque as you like, 'and the whities kicked up a stink about *unsanitary conditions* and the whole place got cleared. And then all the rich white folks got poor when the mining stopped, and cleared-off anyways. Now even the last ones are getting spooked like little girls and running out of town.'

'What do you mean, spooked?' I say.

Paulie looks at me, holds my eye for a moment before he decides to ignore me, turning instead to Pete. 'You met the old codger down the road?' he says. 'Mr Prendergast?'

'You mean in the broken-down house?' Pete says. 'Yeah, funny you should say that. We went across the other day, didn't we, babe? We don't have a phone line yet, so Ali thought it would be good to go down there, see if they're fixed up. Anyway, the old bugger wouldn't come out from behind his door. Shouting at us to clear-off his land. Making out as though he had a gun!' Pete's telling this story like it's a joke, building to a kind of ludicrous finale. Paulie looks nonplussed.

'Yeah,' Paulie says. 'I wouldn't get any closer. He's a nasty piece of work. Kids left years ago and don't come back to visit. People keep hoping he's died up there. Or that they've finally shifted him out to the camps.'

I'm about to ask about whether there's a *Mrs* Prendergast, but now I need to know what he means about the camps. 'What do you mean, shifted him out?' I say. 'You mean to the Internally Displaced Camps? Why would he go to the camps?'

'Oh they're always trying to get us to leave,' Mara says. 'Coming round with their clipboards, telling us it's best to go before there's an emergency.'

'What do you mean?' I ask. 'What kind of emergency?'

Paulie snorts. 'Look at her, getting all riled up,' he says. 'Thought you were meant to be a high-flyer, working for the State an' all,' he says. 'Thought you'd know all about it.'

Even Pete looks a bit perturbed now. 'A'right, mate,' he says. 'Fill us in then.'

'It's nothing,' Mara says, looking up from the baby. She's still got a beatific look in her eyes; she's going to pacify us just like she has Iluka. 'They just don't want to pay for services round here. They've shut down everything they can. They want us all to shift into the camp over in the next territory, so that they don't have to worry about fire protection and proper healthcare. They even offer us money to go, a re-settlement payment. Bribery.'

'No bugger ever comes back from those camps,' Paulie says. 'They're trying to get all of us in public-housing to shift out there, and then there's no tenancy to come back to. Clarence, fella down our street, went out a few months ago, then changed his mind, wanted to come home. They told him he'd have to pay back his compensation money and that there was no housing left for him out here. They've boarded up his house and it's full of pigeons and meth-heads now, poor bugger.'

'Shit,' says Pete. 'I went into town earlier to try to report on the old bloke, what d'you call him, Prendergast? That's when I bumped into you, mate, and– '

'That right?' Paulie says, 'You were trying to report on him in the pub, were you, mate?' He laughs, then knocks back his beer, giving me side-eye.

Pete's very busy not looking at me. 'Yeah, well, before that, mate. I was thinking maybe Social Services, someone might want to know about him. Anyway, couldn't find a single service to report him to. Nearest Social Services office is in the next district, a copper told me, and the medical centre was… well, I didn't get to speak to anyone there either.'

Paulie looks at me straight on now. He puts his beer down and takes a deep sniff. 'So you didn't know anything about this, eh, darl? Services being shut down? All the ockers and Abos being shifted out? Housing Department in the city not behind all this?'

I shake my head. 'Well, I know about ID Camps,' I say. 'And the local council has eviction powers and compensation schemes. And, obviously, they can remove vulnerable people, when they're at risk of being affected by a heat event. No territory is meant to be using them *before* there's a credible threat.'

'Right,' Mara says. 'And there isn't any sort of credible threat here. They just want us gone so they don't have to pay anyone to protect us. So they keep warning us about heat events, and outbreaks that are never going to happen.'

'Outbreaks?' I say. 'What kind of outbreaks?'

'Oh, all sorts of things,' she says, real blasé. 'Asthma, from the fires, which are actually hundreds of miles away. Rabies, they said that was the new threat just a few months back. Now they're saying that skin business. They tell us they don't have the resources for anything except emergencies now, and we should take compensation and move to the camps. That we'll be much safer there, with proper medical facilities.'

'Yeah,' Paulie laughs darkly. 'Folk in camps have always been safe, right?'

'So *that's* why they wouldn't register you at the doctors', babe,' Pete says brightly. 'They're under-resourced. It's nothing to do with cutis.'

'But what about the fires?' I say. 'Maybe there *is* smoke in the air here? And what if there *are* outbreaks of cutis in this area?' I look at Iluka, still asleep in Mara's arms. I see the rise and fall of his little body. How effortful his breathing seems, the little gasp of the in-breath moving his whole torso. He's still just learning to be alive; keep your baby close to you at the beginning, they told us in the classes, so that he can learn to regulate his breathing, so that he can keep his heart beating, patterning his tiny pulse against the thrum of yours. He's still just learning to survive. How can she be so relaxed? 'Aren't you worried?' I say, 'Aren't you worried for him?'

101

'Honestly,' Mara says, 'we've lived here our whole lives and they're always trying to shift us off the land. They're always trying to scare us off with something. The fires never get across the mountains. Even if they look close, even if, technically, they sometimes get close, there's all that rain-forest and rock in the way. Lakoomba hasn't ever burned, not in living memory. And, right enough, people get sick, but people get sick everywhere.'

'The folk they send in, clutching their clipboards and telling us about risk factors, telling us we're classed as *vulnerable*, they're not from round here. They don't understand how this land works,' Paulie says. 'They want us out. I'm telling you, those clipboard cunts who work for the camps, there's something in it for them if they persuade us to go, some sort of sweetener. Now then,' he says, 'where's this good, city shit you mentioned, Petey? We going to have a smoko on your porch?'

Paulie and Mara stayed for hours. The conversation moved on, but I couldn't stop thinking about the camps and the fires and the outbreaks, and, as they talked about bars in the city and gigs and beer recipes, I kept trying to steer us back to the risks, until Pete told me to, 'Change the bloody record, darl,' and Paulie sniggered. When they finally left, Pete said we should hit the sack. 'I know what you're going to do, Ali,' he said. 'I know you're going to want to pick through everything they said and decide what you're going to get most freaked out about. I'm tired and liquored-up, babe. Let's try to get some shut-eye.'

And now I can't sleep. Again. I lie on my back in bed, listening to the house settling down into the not-quite-dark night. Pete is wet with sweat beside me and humming periodically. He turns suddenly, his legs kicking out as though he's falling, and then he drops, heavy and still. I lift the sheet to try to let some air across my skin. It's so hot that I feel like I'm tightening up. The skin on my stomach is running all over with burning, electrical sensations. I must not scratch. I must not scratch. I remember a woman at one of our antenatal classes who must have been as far gone as I am now. Impossibly large, she'd seemed at the time. She'd let go, she said, she just couldn't hold back anymore, and we all thought she was talking about eating – she'd gained a fair amount of weight – but then she'd lifted her peach smock and all over her swollen, low stomach were deep, livid scratch marks. They'd grazed in some places, and you could see where the old blood was crusting over, and where she kept on opening herself back up. 'I've had to cut my nails right down,' she said, and lowered her shirt. 'Calamine,' the course leader said, 'and self-discipline.' The rest of us were still staring, open-mouthed.

I've got to get more air. I get up from the bed and go over to the window, trying to jam it up even further. It's already open as far as it will go. I look out over the garden. Something outside is ticking away in the bushes. There's a slight breeze through the jarrah, but the air's warm and thick. Nothing's going to bring relief from the heat.

I lie awake, or half-awake, for hours. I'm so hot I wonder if I'm starting with a fever. I listen to my heart beating, hard and unpredictable. I suppose Pete's right: I'm the strange one, thinking about it all the time. Pete is the normal one, assimilating cutis to the list of everyday risks, just like Mara and Paulie and everyone else. For them, it's just one other thing adding to a background hum of distant dangers, a fading anxiety-drone: melanoma, heat events, cutis. Wear sun-block, avoid danger spots, get treatment. But, back when it first started, I wasn't the only one interested in the details: there were news reports, every day, and all of the big networks ran features. I've catalogued most of them, in my files. A small mountain town in Peru, the site of an American smelting company, had a well-documented outbreak. In the TV news report, a young man, wearing a bright orange tracksuit, sits on a rocky outcrop in front of an industrial tower. He grins straight at the camera, seeming to enjoy the attention. He gestures dramatically, makes his hands into fists and places them against his ears; then he hurls his hands outwards explosively, fingers splayed, miming an eruption from his head. The translator tells us that the man had gone to sleep one night, his ears perfectly normal. He woke up in the night to a terrible itching, like something was burrowing into the skin around his ears, and when he tried to scratch himself, he felt something there, something *in* his ears. And he knew immediately that it was the 'Skin Worms'. The reporter tells us that this is the local term for cutis. In the boy's village, more than ten people have been affected in the last two months. The boy proudly shows his ears to the camera: there are welts along the curved folds of his inner ear, cauterised wounds that are still glistening red in places, but they are scabbing over, forming a black crust at the edges. It still itches, the boy says cheerfully, but now he knows he will be able to hear. The doctors were kind and the smelting company gave his father money for new clothes and medicines, he says. He gives a double thumbs-up to the camera.

Another report focused on a large number of women living in a village along the Citarum river in Indonesia. The reporter wears a mask as she walks along the side of the Citarum and describes the geography of the area and the large proportion of women affected. The Citarum river is the most polluted body of water in the world, she tells us, that's why she's wearing the mask; but the children who occasionally run across her path have wide-open mouths, gaping delightedly as they dash in and out of shot. The river doesn't appear to move at all as the reporter walks alongside it: it's covered over with greyish debris, a barely-drifting scurf of different bits of plastic. In occasional patches, close to the side of the river, the debris clears inexplicably, revealing still ovals of black water. The reporter is wearing a linen suit, and she moves her hands as she walks. Her voice is only slightly muffled by the mask. The Citarum is the longest river in West Java, she tells us, and 7 million people live in its basin. Large textile factories further downstream are major toxic waste contributors, and the river contains high levels of lead, mercury and arsenic. The rice paddies that used to surround the river have stopped producing food, poisoned beyond productivity. The land has been sold-off at rock-bottom prices to hydro-electricity firms. The report cuts to the inside of a village house. Several women sit in a circle. Some are elderly, their faces grave and tired. A young woman has a baby tied to her front with a bright blue piece of cloth. She cradles him, and her mouth is flat, dimpled at the edges in disappointment, or distaste, or surgical reconfiguration. The women begin to speak in turn, and their words are dubbed over with a young woman's voice in English. 'I didn't know what was happening,' one older woman is saying, in her own voice and then in the young translator's voice. 'I felt sick and tired. That is not so unusual. The river has always given me headaches. Then one night I went to bed and the skin around my nose became itchy. I rubbed at it, but I couldn't get at the itch. And I could feel something growing there. When I woke my husband he shouted, and pushed me away. I went to a friend, and her son took me to see a doctor the next day and he treated me for cutis. I have no children,' the woman says, looking miserably at the floor, 'and my husband will not have me back in the house. There is no one to look after me except for my friend.' The woman begins to weep and another comforts her. The woman's nose has been reopened, but the surgery looks basic: the nostrils are bullish, outlined in red, crude circles newly produced by the cauterisation.

These reports kept on coming for a while, and the most hard-hitting were the ones where the symptoms were caught on camera. I've archived footage of a Sri Lankan woman whose mouth was lost in folds of crinkled skin, filmed just before her surgery; of two Bolivian children, brothers, whose ears were muffled in a new epidermis. And the horror stories of ad-hoc surgeries, of hideous mishaps and infections, I've saved those too. Gradually the stories stopped coming. And people in the city seemed to forget all about it. And people are still forgetting, people like Pete who might have seen symptoms just this morning. Is it mad to think about cutis all the time, to document its effects, to think about the people it's claimed, the people it's sealing in right now? Or is it madness to sleep soundly, forgetting all about the very thing that might seal you into your own dreams?

My mother's the last thing I think about, she's the last thing I try to shut out, before I finally drift into a fitful sleep.

V

WHEN I wake up, Pete's already downstairs, banging about in the kitchen. It takes a while for the feeling of my dreams to clear; the details have already melted away again, but there's a bad atmosphere left behind, like a colour filter across my thinking. I try to shake it off. I sit up in bed and bend my legs, attempting to get comfortable around the bump. The window's still wide open and I can feel a breeze. It's blissful. I lean my head backwards, letting my neck stretch.

'Sleeping Beauty,' Pete's voice says. He's at the bedroom door, holding a tray.

'What time is it?' I ask.

'It's nearly midday. I didn't want to wake you. You must've needed the rest.' He places the tray down on the bed next to me. 'Toast? *Protected* juice?'

I don't feel hungry, but I'm so thirsty that I grab the juice and gulp it down. Too quickly, it's too quickly, and it won't go down properly and I can practically feel the heartburn already, but I need so badly to drink it. I finish the glass and then lean my head backwards again.

'It *rained*,' Pete says, with such earnestness that I can't help but smile. It's as though it's the first time he's seen precipitation; he might as well have said it *snowed* for all the incredulity in his voice.

'Really?' I say and I pat the bed for him to sit down beside me.

'Yep, first thing this morning. Well, it was almost rain. Drizzle, really. I watched it from the verandah. Babe, it was beautiful. The mountains got even bluer and then they disappeared completely. It lasted about half-an-hour. And now everything smells different. It's so fresh out there.' He leans back against the headboard too, taking his Greek coffee, sipping it so that the foam briefly collects on his upper lip then melts away. 'I knew it was the right thing,' he says. 'Coming out here. I knew it.' He reaches out with one hand and rests it on my belly. 'I can't wait to show this one the bush.'

We sit like that for a while and I look out at the sky: it's a strange colour, a kind of mottled violet-yellow, like a fading bruise. I put my hand up to my fringe: I can feel the frizz in my hair, and there's a kind of soft fizz on the air too, a prickle of electricity.

'What are you going to do today?' Pete asks.

'I'm going to get us some curtains,' I say, deciding it there and then.

'Yeah?' Pete says. 'Top idea. Do you want me to come?'

'No,' I say. 'It'll be good for me to get out on my own. I can't sleep with all this light.'

'You seemed to sleep fine this morning,' he says. 'You were snoring like a pregnant buffalo.' He pushes his face into my hair and nuzzles my neck. 'I love you, Ali,' he whispers.

'Yeah, alright,' I say.

I make my adjustments to the car seat again and get into my strange new driving position. Everything looks different today, now that the sky is full of this sharp, changeable light. The little houses on the edge of town look more desolate, the yellow-cast making them less picturesque and more jaundiced. There are gardenias in and amongst the wild flowers at the edge of the road and all of the heavy orange flowers are shivering in the breeze. The sky's darker over towards the mountains. This might be the moment before the storm: that moment when the world seems tender, everything drawn together, everything flinching at once, before the sky opens.

I find a parking spot in town. I've no idea where to get curtains: there aren't any of the big shops from the city out here. I wander up the main street, peering in windows. There's an old grocery store that's selling second-hand mobile phones and games consoles; there are a few vacant properties; there's a discount frozen-goods store, with water pooling in one aisle and a strong smell of rotting fish drifting out the door. At the top of the street there's a small dry-cleaners shop. The peeling paint on the window says that they also do alterations, repairs and 'curtains made'. I step inside. There's a strong smell of cleaning chemicals, sweet and sickly like marker pens; the air is circulated around the place by a fan, which turns slowly, this way and that, on the counter-top. I don't want to spend long in here, not without my face-mask. I try to breathe as little as possible. There's no air-con and the two heavily made-up women who sit at sewing machines behind the counter look like they're in a chemical stupor. They're both older than me, one in her late fifties, maybe, hair scooped back in a net, fat red lips, her orange face interrupted with tiny blisters of sweat. The other looks older; she's thick around the middle, with a short, blonde helmet of curls. She stares at me, and at my belly, then gets up with evident reluctance.

'Yeah?' she says. 'What can I do you for?' She leans on the counter. Her skin is dark brown, over-tanned, and on her shoulders the sun-spots are seared together. Some of them are speckled with black.

'I'd like to get some curtains made up,' I say.

'Yeah?' she says. 'What fabric?'

'Oh,' I say. 'I don't have any fabric. Can I buy fabric here?'

'Nope,' the woman says. 'We can't make you curtains without any fabric. We're not magicians.'

'Stop busting her balls!' the other woman shouts from the back. She gets up from behind her machine and comes to the front, barging the older woman out of the way.

'You can see she's in some trouble,' the orange woman says. 'You're carrying nice and high. How far along are you, darl?'

'Um, thirty-six weeks,' I say. 'Almost thirty-seven.'

'Ah,' she says. 'Little one's almost here.' Little one? My stomach twists. I start to gag on the chemicals.

'And you've just moved out here? To this backwater? Christ, what was you thinking?'

'I'm just trying to get some curtains,' I say. 'Can't sleep for the light.'

'Yeah, she looks tired, don't she, Jules?'

Jules has returned to the back of the shop. She grunts and then leans down to fiddle with the peddle of her machine.

'Well, we can't do much without fabric. The old haberdashery shut down last year. You might have some luck with the bric-a-brac store down the end of the street. You know the one? Right at the bottom? No telling exactly what they'll have, but they sometimes get a load of cotton in. So long as you're not fussy about the pattern.'

'I'm not fussy,' I say.

'Good girl,' she says. 'You come back with some fabric and we'll fix you up a treat.'

A bell rings as I leave the shop and both machines whir back into life.

'They're thick as shit, coming out here,' I hear Jules say, just as the door swings closed, 'Last thing we need is bloody wogs from the city.'

I go back to the bottom of the street, to the store I think the woman described. It's the old fish market, now stocked-up with piles of miscellaneous merchandise: a wall full of tinned spam, a pile of netted bags with flimsy-looking, miniature tennis rackets inside, t-shirts in day-glo colours with fake plastic logos. I can't see anyone else in the store and I'm about to give up when I spot a high shelf with some long rolls of fabric. I reach up, and there's a sharp tearing sensation through the skin of my stomach. I lean over and pant for a while, wrapping my stomach in my arms. I look back up at the fabric. None of it looks right anyway. There's a fluffy fake-fur in bright orange. A violet gauze with a gold pattern running through it. And a thick blue cotton, with white, embossed flowers. I can practically smell the toxicity from here. God knows what it's printed with; the whole shop stinks like new trainers, plastic and poisonous.

When I leave the shop, I can't stop myself. I'm so close by that I have to check on the doctors' surgery, just to see if the queues are still as bad, just to see if there's an obvious pattern to the symptoms down here. I turn the corner and the street is quiet. The sky is darker overhead now, and something shifts in the breeze: a paper bag cartwheeling in the gutter. There's no queue at all. In fact there's no one on the street at all. I walk right up to the surgery door. All of the handwritten signs have been removed; just the drawing pins have been left behind, little tears of paper tacked under the brass circles. Perhaps the rush of symptoms is over? Perhaps there'll be a midwife who's able to see me now? I turn the door handle, carefully, just wanting to peek inside. It doesn't budge.

'They've gone.' The voice is far off. I turn around and I can't see anyone on the street. 'They've relocated,' the voice calls again, 'to the camp. Over in the next territory.' It takes me a while to spot him. Everything on the street seems to be sliding, the shadows lengthening quickly as the sky moves in ripples of light. He's sitting on the pavement, a few yards away from me, under the awning of an empty shop. It's the man without shoes. The blackfella with the ambiguous toes. I step closer to him.

'Gone?' I say. 'What do you mean gone?' I take another step closer. I want to get close enough to see his feet.

'Not enough of 'em left,' he says. 'To deal with all the sick.'

I'm close to him now. He shifts suddenly, folding his feet away underneath him.

'What do you mean? Sick with what? Sick with cutis? Are *you* ok?' I ask. 'Are your feet ok? Were you trying to get treated?'

'I don't need your help,' he says. 'Pfff.' He looks up at me. He makes his eyes small and he studies my face, and then my stomach. He laughs. 'You're the one that needs help, little melon.'

I've almost got my key in the car-door when the first fat, warm drops of rain begin to fall. They spatter on the ground, like little bleeds across the dusty tarmac. I don't rush at first. I just stand there, letting the wetness soak into the back of my t-shirt. It's good to feel it, something cool against my skin. The rain is getting heavier, so I let myself into the driver's seat and fall back behind the wheel. By the time I get to the edge of town it's falling so hard that it's difficult to see the road. The rain is bouncing off the street and there are foamy rivers beginning to gush at the edges of the pavement. I drive extra slowly. Every so often something appears through the deluge: a pair of girls, rushing across the road, clutching a disintegrating newspaper over their heads; a woman pushing a sodden baby in a pram, its big mouth hinging into a red squall. When I turn onto our road I'm driving so slowly that

I'm barely moving. I can just about make out the outline of the old man's house, old Prendergast, as I crawl alongside it, and a fork of lightning momentarily illumines the scene: the sky is violet, a dense, sickly hue; the house beneath it is being lashed, the white wood re-cast in dark grey, the roof and verandah running with grey water. The long grass is completely flattened in places and I see that mangy old cat, bent low, frozen; and then there's the thunder clap and everything fades back into milky obscurity.

In the dash from the car to the front-door, I get completely soaked. Even my shoes are filled with water. Pete comes through from the kitchen to see me shaking-off; he laughs out-loud, then coos.

'Poor bub,' he says. 'Bad timing.'

'We're not getting curtains,' I say.

'That right?' he says.

'I've heard that natural light is better for your sleep-patterns, anyhow. Something to do with the circadian rhythm.'

'Whatever you say, babe.'

'I'm going to get cleaned up,' I say.

Upstairs I peel my wet clothes off, hanging them out in the bathroom to dry. My legs and feet are all gritty, so I step into the shower. Who knows what's in the rainwater: aluminium, barium, magnesium, at the very least. I scrub at my skin with a brush. I pick up the protected shower oil and squeeze a large amount into my hands, so that it runs through my fingers. I rub it all over my skin, as far down my legs as I can reach. And then I massage it over my stomach. I feel something hard at the bottom right-hand side, just below the surface, a small elbow, perhaps, or the front of a tiny skull. I try, I really do try to think of a baby inside me, a *little one*. It's so implausible: instead, I picture fossils, the strange, curved bones of ancient reptiles, patterned inside soft mudstone. I stay in the shower until I've drained the hot-water tank and the water runs cold.

When I get downstairs, Pete's opened a beer and is pacing up and down in front of the open window.

'Come look,' he says. 'It's beautiful.'

''Suppose you've finished work for the day, then?' I say.

'I reckon.'

It's still raining outside, a soft gauze over the garden, but the centre of the storm has moved off. We watch lightning flash over the mountains, and then – one Mississippi, two Mississippi, three – the clap of thunder. When the sky lights up the mountains look especially blue: an unreal, smoky cobalt under the greenish-purple storm-sky.

Pete is excited. 'I haven't seen a storm like this in yonks,' he says. 'Do you remember, Ali, that night when we were kids when we stole out and took the monorail around the city, and the heavens opened and you thought we were going to be electrocuted?' Pete laughs and puts his arm around me. I remember the night he's talking about. We must have been about sixteen. Pete had nicked a bottle of red wine from his dad, and we ran down the street and jumped on the train together, no clear idea of where we would go. As the train rose up on the overhead track we could see the sky, dark as ink, on the other side of the city. We got closer and closer, the train and the sky moving inexorably towards one another, and then the storm broke above us, shuddering down rain, convulsing with green light. The lightning flashed up bits of the city I'd never seen before: the massive factories and refineries to the north, the surrounding scrubland, a ragged family of red foxes cowering in a swathe of bottle-brush. We didn't get off the train. Pete opened the bottle of wine with his Swiss Army knife and we glugged it back until our lips and teeth were black. It was driverless, the monorail, on a loop around the same corner of the city. We sat right at the front, as though it was a roller-coaster, and I squealed, grabbing Pete every time the thunder rolled. At each stop, bedraggled folk got on, wiping their faces and shaking-off their umbrellas. And when it was their stop they hunched against the storm, dashing out and running for cover.

I used to like being a little bit frightened with Pete, I guess. It was part of my and Pete's friendship. He'd introduce me to things that were beyond my ken; I had no extended family, no older siblings or cousins, to open up the world for me. I'd always protest about where he was taking me, but I loved the places in the city that he knew about, and the things we used to do together. Pete had brothers and cousins and an endless supply of secret, terrifying locations that they'd introduced him to. The abandoned sugar refinery at the edge of town, where he'd go to play guitar and smoke dope. The underground car-park in the centre of the city that turned into a sleazy party zone at night. The old abattoir, its yard a mess of broken glass and weeds, in the ruins of which we'd build fires, the boys daring one another to break in, to run through the metal hooks and reappear from the other end of the building. We'd all scream outside like stuck pigs whenever anyone took the challenge, whinnying and snorting, acting out being slaughtered. I guess we all liked playing at being frightened, back then, trying out fear like an exotic accent. And after the fear had passed, we'd bunch together again, jittery but safe.

Pete and me, we messed around when we were kids, all adrenaline and furious pashing. Things didn't get serious until later on. It was the year after college. I'd just started in the Department of Housing and had moved back in with Mum for a few months, to save for a deposit so that I could rent a room in the city. I hated being home: Mum's cooking, her TV habits, the way she had things laid out in the bathroom, everything about her annoyed me at close quarters. Her generosity ('I can do that for you; let me...'), her gentle enquiries about where I'd be on a given evening, her sweet voice-messages on my work line about the garden, all of it I hated. One night I was sitting out back, in an ungrateful sulk, drinking wine, and I saw a man laughing in the lit-up flat next door, drinking beer with a beautiful girl. What's that man doing in Eleni and John's flat, I wondered? And before I could answer the question he turned to look out of the window, saw me, paused. It was Pete. He didn't smile, exactly; it was something more guarded. He acknowledged me, looked at me expectantly, waiting for me to acknowledge him. And then he came out back. The girl in the kitchen turned and stared at the open door.

'Alice,' he said. 'It's been an age.' He looked different. He held himself differently; he'd grown up, late in the day, his pudgy face toughening, his body broadening. He was handsome and proud of himself. 'What you doing back?' he asked.

'Staying with my mum for a bit,' I said. It was strange seeing him again. I was pleased to see him, sure I was, yet I felt a little shiver of hostility towards him too, and I realised that even though we were friends, even though we'd been more than friends, I'd always envied him. That was it. I felt a little stab of envy, because, even though they slept two to a bed next-door and fought over food, he had always had his siblings and his family full of cousins and uncles and aunties, and a mother and a father who adored him. I was envious of his chubby cheeks, and the way he knew how to receive love from my mother and everyone else around him: greedily, without guilt. And now, I was envious of the way he was at home again, looking so easy in his parents' kitchen as someone new adored him. There would always be someone staring at a doorway Pete had just walked through, hoping he'd return. The woman in the kitchen looked out as us still.

I felt something other than envy, too: a new curiosity, as he looked at me, about what he'd become.

'Will you come for a drink with me, Ali?' he asked.

'You've got company,' I said.

'Nah,' he said. 'She's going.'

'What a gent,' I said.

It's strange to be told that someone is in love with you when you're an introvert. How can you be in love with me, I thought. What bit of the tiny sliver of myself that I allowed to escape can possibly have given you enough grounds for love? Sure, we'd been friends. At times we'd been more than friends. But I'd stayed guarded; when we played together, when we'd pashed as teenagers, even when we'd messed around. How could he possibly think he loved me? Pete declared it over and over again that summer. That first night, when we drank ourselves stupid in an empty bar at the edge of our estate, then walked home along the dark streets, laughing and bumping into one another, standing in front of the flats, kissing each other while the world seemed to spin around us – it was the world that was drunk, not us, we were the still bright centre for the whirling stars overhead and the lopsided cats that weaved around us and the distant cars and someone, far off, shouting again and again 'Maria, Maaaarrrrriiiiiaaaa' – all of it span around us while we burned into one another, bright and hot. And I sneaked him upstairs into my old bedroom, and we kissed and kissed till our lips were sore, and then we moved onto the floor so as not to make the bed moan and he poured the words into my ear: 'I love you, I love you, Alice, I've always loved you.'

He declared it again, every time we met. Sometimes as soon as we met: outside a bar or a restaurant, he'd greet me and kiss my face and say straight away, as though the world was ending and we had only minutes left, 'I love you, Ali, I love you, I love you.' He said it until I believed it, until I felt it too. I'd always been guarded, not just with Pete, with other blokes too, but now something inside me broke away, painfully. I remember my mother once told me that there are plants in the bush that have adapted to survive the wild fires: their buds burst into seed only through flames. That's what it felt like: I was on fire, exploding into life. And finally I said it, the words burst out of me too: 'I love you,' I said. 'I love you, Pete.' And I felt it, hot and wild and painful.

We started making plans. Pete was living in a filthy shared-house in a bad part of the city. He'd done a course on design and was trying to find work, taking up anything he could while he worked up a portfolio. He worked all kinds of jobs to stay afloat, horrible jobs, and they never lasted long. He took night shifts in a bottle factory at the edge of the outback, until all the summer workers got laid off. Then he worked on a demolition site, where the safety procedures were sketchy at best and the gaffer made everyone work their first fortnight without pay, 'To reimburse the company for your equipment, mate.' Pete stayed at that one until he almost fell: he'd been edging along a rafter when a pigeon shat on his face. Then he found a job working behind a bar, at a place on the right side of town for our estate. This was the best gig he'd had by far. Said he'd move back home too, and we could both save up and look for an apartment to rent together in the city.

I didn't go to the bar he worked at that much. I was commuting everyday anyway, working hard to impress Kim and to earn a permanent post at the Department. And I didn't like to cramp Pete's style: he looked shy whenever I did go in, and I guessed it must be awkward for him to serve me. One evening Pete's bar was hosting a festival: local bands in the car-park, food-stalls, buckets full of ice and beer, that kind of thing. Pete's brother knocked on our door, suggested we go down together. It was nice to walk across the estate with Harris: it was Friday night, weekly payday for folks with jobs, so everyone out had a swagger to their step. A couple of lads whistled hellos to us from across the road and the high-rises at the centre of St Paul's were hazed in bronze light, so that even they looked kind of pretty. Windows were open, music was playing, people were running their mouths and laughing. Harris had grown up too: he'd been a giddy boy, liable to start fires and shoplift. Now he was training to be a nurse, and he held my hand, careful and protective, as we laced through the blocks towards the city.

The place was rammed when we arrived, so it took us a while to spot Pete, serving beers from behind a table at the far end of the car-park, just under the flyover. There was a punk band playing and the traffic roared overhead. Pete didn't look exactly pleased to see us. He patted Harris on the arm, gave me a kiss on the cheek.

'It's so busy,' he said, slipping us a couple of free beers under the table. 'I don't think I'm going to get a break till we finish up at midnight, babe. You two go listen to the bands, enjoy yourselves.'

Harris downed his beer and got straight down the front, doing this strange little dance of his: when Harris dances, he bends repeatedly, suddenly tipping his torso forward with alarming rapidity. I milled about the edges of the circle of moshing kids, watching Pete from a distance. Everyone seemed to know him; regulars I guessed.

I got another free beer and bought some shots. I danced a bit on my own. I chatted to an older guy who was high and wanted us to go for a walk together, 'Off under the flyover and into the sunset.' I laughed. Said I needed to powder my nose and gave him the slip.

The loos were full of discarded bottles and girls chattering aggressively, sharing stalls and hatching plans for the rest of the night.

'Let's go on to Tony's.'

'I don't want to. He's a bloody bore.'

'Yeah, but he'll have ket, and I know he likes you. He'll be generous with it.'

'So what's that, darl? You trying to pimp me out to get your pills?'

Laughter. Clattering. Laughter.

I was just about to flush when another pair started up in the stall next door.

'Don't you fancy him?'

'What, Pete?'

'Yeah. He was all over you, babe. And he can't stop looking at you.'

'I guess he's good looking. But I think he's sort of creepy.'

'Really? I think he's hot.'

'Nah. He's got a girlfriend. And he's slept with every other girl who works behind the bar. Lindsey had a thing with him, a bit ago. Says he can get nasty.'

'What do you mean, nasty?'

'Like, wild. Really pushy. And then wants nothing to do with you.'

'Well, do you mind if try him out? I could do with a bit of nasty, tonight.'

'Be my guest, babe. Just don't come crying to me when he goes back to his childhood sweetheart. And you better make sure you stay safe. That guy is reckless.'

My heart is beating hard in my chest. I hear their stall door clatter open, and I follow them out a couple of seconds later. I loiter beside them at the basins, sprinkling my hands with water while they gum up their lips with more gloss. I vaguely recognise one of them: she's got long red hair and I guess I must have seen her behind the bar. I keep my head down, so she won't recognise me. The other girl is tall and blonde with extremely assertive tits, which she pushes up inside her bra. I trail them out of the loos and watch as they make their way towards Pete. I sit down on the banking at the edge of the car-park, trying to make myself inconspicuous. The sky is navy-blue now and the air is cooling quickly. Multi-coloured lights are strung-up around the edges of car-park, but I'm a way back from them and must be pretty well hidden in the darkness. Pete looks delighted to see the girls: he barrels out his chest, slips them drinks too. The Amazonian blonde is sidling up to him. I see him do a quick sweep of the surroundings, presumably looking for me. He scans the crowd in front of him once, twice, and then he relaxes, steps back from the table with the girl, lights her cigarette. I sit a while longer, watching as Pete and the girl dance around each other, their bodies getting closer and closer, Pete getting more and more tense. The girl cups her hand around his ear, presses her body against him, whispers something. He keeps checking around, and he looks kind of agitated, in a nervous-excited way. I see him glance around once more, and then he moves quickly in a fuck-it, let's-do-it kind of a way: he grabs the girl by the wrist, practically spins her round, and yanks her off into the darkness under the flyover.

I tell Harris that I'm leaving. 'Righto,' he says, then carries on dancing. I melt into the darkness, out towards the city. I walk across the flyover, and the dancing kids below, and the roar of traffic underneath me, and whatever Pete and that girl are doing, feel further and further away. There's a breeze up here, and the stars are glinting, and I feel very, very sharp. I'm an arrow ready to be shot into the night sky.

I keep walking along the main roads. The traffic thins out and a car full of boys slows down next to me.

'A'right, darl, you want to come and party with us?'

'Come on you beaut, come on in and keep us company.'

'Give us a smile then, ya bloody sour-faced bitch.'

I keep on walking and their insults blare into noise as they drive past.

In town, it's chucking-out time and people are stumbling around, feeling their way along walls, supporting one another. I find a little cellar bar that I've been to before with Pete that's open late. I sit at the bar and I order shots. I feel so purposeful-but-purposeless, so full of restless angry energy, that I think I might burst. A guy sits beside me at the bar and offers to buy me a drink. He's tall, an enormous American, with a soft voice and a crucifix tattooed up the side of his thick neck. While he's introducing himself I start kissing him. I don't stop. I take him by the hand and lead him out into the city. I lead him down an alleyway and lace my arms around the back of his neck. He smells so clean and so new. I try to be wild and reckless, but I start to cry.

'Listen,' he says. 'You're real cute, and real drunk. If you still want to do this in the morning, you give me a call.'

He writes his number on a piece of paper and hails me a taxi. That's when I find out his name, as I unfurl the scrap of paper in the back of the Falcon, the lights fading out as we drive back towards the estate: Patrick.

When I get back to my mum's, Pete's asleep in my bed. I keep my clothes on and I get in beside him. He murmurs in his sleep.

'I saw you,' I say, drunkenly pushing my lips against his scalp.

He doesn't hear me; he wraps his arms around me instinctively in his sleep.

'I saw you.'

The next morning we had it out properly. Pete looked stunned, genuinely injured that I was bringing it up.

'Babe,' he said, 'it's absolutely nothing. It was just a quick chat with a pissed-up girl. I love you, Alice, you know that I love you. Anyway, I thought we were alright with extras? We talked about it, you said it was fine.'

It was true: we had talked about it. We'd both said we weren't that fussed about monogamy, that we were young and we should make the most of it. But we'd said it in bed, hypothetically, with our legs laced together. We hadn't talked about details. I thought that was for the future; I didn't realise it was now.

'Were you safe?' I asked, over and over again. 'Have you been safe, with every single one?'

Of course he hadn't been safe. I knew it the moment he paused before answering.

'Lydia's a good girl,' he said. 'You don't need to worry.'

'Lydia?'

We went at it for a long time: I wanted every single

person, I wanted personal histories and risks taken. There were many: many women and many risks. He had his head in his hands by the end. 'Alice,' he said. 'I'm sorry. I don't know how to explain it to ya. It's like, because I love you so much, there's too much of it. It makes me fall in love with everyone, just a little bit. I'll stop, I'll stop. I can stop. Just tell me to.'

The strange thing is, I sort of understood. I know that fire spreads. I'd felt it too, the too-muchness of being in love. But I hated Pete for it at the same time. I hated his freedom and how guiltlessly he lived, how easily he took love and gave love, and how much danger he'd put me in. And most of all, I hated that he might be right, that he was living the right way and that I was wrong: too frightened, too careful, too guarded to really enjoy life. I didn't have the constitution for it: I couldn't live like him, it was too much, it was too reckless for me, and I should have known and I should never have said I love you, I love you too, I should never have tried to love like he did, wide open and wild.

Pete's still staring at the sky above the mountains. 'Hey babe,' he says. 'You're miles away. Don't you remember? The monorail, the storm that night?'

'I remember,' I say.

And I do remember, I think of us again as fifteen-year olds, clinging together under the big sky. But what I'm thinking is: you can't fall in love twice. Not even with the same person. After the first flames, everything is just dying sparks.

VI

WE'RE going out tonight,' Pete says. We're sitting on the verandah eating breakfast. Pete is stuffing toast and peanut butter into his mouth, talking while he chews. The sky is clear and whitish-blue beyond us. The storm has cleared and everything in the garden looks fresh. There's that warm smell of earth, after the rain; an almost animal smell, like clean, soft cat fur. 'Petrichor.' My mother's words in my mind again.

'Are we?' I say.

'Yeah. Paulie and Mara are having a barbie tonight. Be a good way to meet some more of the locals.'

'Right,' I say. 'Maybe you'd have a better time without me.' If I go I won't be able to stop myself from quizzing people, from asking them about any suspected cases and about the risk of fire here. And Pete will go ape. And then there's the barbie itself: blackened, carcinogenic, unprotected meat; formaldehyde fumes; people smoking.

'You're coming, Alice,' Pete says. 'I'm not having you hiding yourself away, becoming some kind of maternal recluse. You liked Mara, right? And you'll want friends when the baby's here.'

'Right,' I say.

Pete works all day and I mill about the house, listless. When I get too hot I step out onto the verandah. It's even warmer out here and my back's killing me, so I take a short circuit around the garden. Moving around seems to make my back feel easier. I trail my fingers across the leaves of the plants in the borders, searching for something that feels cool. I should probably water them; I've got so used to the water-curfews in the city that it didn't even occur to me. Maybe I can keep things alive out here, finally learn the skills that my mother tried to teach me before everything died back in the city? The vivid violet bush, here at the bottom of the yard, is a jacaranda, I know that much. Next to it is something I don't recognise. I squat down. It's a small, scrubby bush, with dark leaves and tiny pink flowers. The pattern of the petals is real delicate: five cerise leaves with a lighter centre, intricate as a snowflake. The leaves at the bottom of the bush are turning yellow and crispy. I should do something for it, work out what it needs. I've kept some of my mother's old gardening books. They'll be in one of the boxes in the living-room, I can picture us packing them up with the other books. I waddle back inside and fish around in one of the half-unpacked boxes we've left stacked against the wall, a placeholder for these bookshelves Pete's going to build. I find them under a stash of Pete's old comics. Mum loved gardening. We only had a small patch out back, but she made the most of it. Our place was built in the 1950s, a two-bedroom lower maisonette on what was then a shiny new public-housing estate. I know we were lucky, just the two of us in our place, and we were at the end of the block so we got to use the land at the side too – Pete's family had to fit the six of them into the same space next-door, and they ran around in a yard half the size of ours. Mum was always busy out there, when I was small. She'd walk me round the yard, telling me what she'd done that day, which plants she'd separated, which she'd supported, which she was letting go to seed. She built raised beds along the edges of the yard, planting them with veggies. She had climbers on trellises, figs and grapes and roses. She trained growers up the walls of the flat, too, honeysuckle and hydrangea, so it always smelt sweet in the summer. She tried to grow trees in tubs, peppermint and peach, paperbarks and floodgums. I never took to it, the garden, never wanted to get my hands dirty, but when Pete was still young she'd set him on with some task – weeding around the gourds, picking out slugs and dropping them into cups of beer – and he'd be utterly rapt. He'd come in hours later, fingers and face filthy, and sometimes he'd fall asleep on her shoulder as she read to him. She did her best, even later on, to keep things going, even when the summers got too hot and the smogs too toxic, when everything got scorched and had already begun to die back. She spritzed the leaves of her gum trees, she watered every night, she improvised nets out of old curtains to protect her veggies from the air. And she never complained, my mother, when things went wrong. When she lost another job, when she didn't get her Child Support, when the man she'd been seeing suddenly disappeared, when the city started to die and her blue gum crackled to death. It was almost as though she expected these small calamities. A little half-sigh, and then she'd be back to work, checking the small ads for jobs, making stews from frozen meat, busily planting seeds in yoghurt pots on the kitchen windowsill.

She'd left things behind that were worse than our boiling city, I knew that much: she was born to Methodists in the north of that little grey island half-way across the world. Born into cold skies and punishment, she said, and not much else. I asked her, more than once, about her folks. About why we never saw them, why they never visited or wrote. About why I'd never met my grandparents. In my memory of one of these conversations it's summer, a weekend day. She's been working in the yard and has grilled mackerel fillets on the barbecue for our lunch. I'm young, young enough to still ask these questions about her family without realising they might be painful; or without caring if they are. We sit on the garden wall, the wall that she built herself with sand and cement to make a raised-bed for her veggies, she sits there in the sunshine wearing a dirty pinafore, and I say, 'Why don't your mum and dad come to see our yard? Why don't we *know* them? Don't they want to meet me?' That last question would have cost me something, even that young, to say out loud. I can't remember what prompted it that day. Maybe I could hear other families in their own backyards, maybe I could hear kids playing with their siblings, or their cousins, kids who had aunts and uncles and grandparents. Kids who had fathers. Kids who had a proper family, instead of this claustrophobic twosome; kids who came from somewhere they knew about, instead of seeming to appear, like I did, immaculate, out of nothing.

My mother pauses a while to think about my question, turning the idea of her folks over in her mind. She was ever so pretty, my mother, in a way that I often used to resent, because it made her vulnerable. She was small and soft, and she got more beautiful as she aged, because she was crumpled and spoiled in a picturesque way, like an old silk dress that had been screwed up in a corner; or a flower, flattened to silk between the pages of a book, that looks like it might turn to dust on your fingers. Her eyes were bright and fringed with skin as soft as moth's wings, closing when she smiled; her cheeks were high and pink and blotched all over with sun spots; her hair was bleached to baby fluff. She wore exhaustion ever so sweetly. I got to realise that a certain kind of man liked this look: the kind who liked to have already won a fight before it happened; the kind who never did have time to come into the house to meet her daughter or stick around long enough to help build a wall; the kind who disappeared, like my father.

'They aren't *bad* people,' my mother says, still chewing on the idea of her folks. 'I don't want you to think that. Your grandmother,' she says, 'worked in a carpet factory all her life. First female foreman. She was ferocious. Supported the lot of us. Your grandfather,' she says, 'is riddled with arthritis. They aren't *bad* people. It's just, your grandma fought so hard for what we had, it made her mean-spirited. Made her treat everything like a fight, every little thing. She was terrified we'd lose the house that she'd worked so hard to buy from the government, that front step that she scrubbed every Saturday, the hospital bed that she'd managed to get for Dad to sleep on in the front room. If she stopped working, or cleaning, or guarding us all for a moment... It's hard to explain it,' Mum says, looking at me. 'They're not *bad* people, but it's better for us not to be near them.' She blows her fringe out of her face, looks away from me. '*Once*, your grandmother beat me for laughing. I'd run home from school along the canal in the valley bottom, and the air was warm, the first bit of spring sunshine, and the magnolia flowers were forking in the branches of the tree on the corner of our road and I felt giddy, and I burst through into the kitchen and laughed and laughed. I must have been about twelve years old, just a little older than you. "What's funny?" your grandmother said. "Tell me what you're laughing at?" And I had no reason, so I just carried on laughing in her face. And she looks at me in horror, and she says, "You're hysterical, Margery," and then she goes to find a gooseberry cane and she comes back and she whips me with it, across the backs of my legs.' My mother leans her head back, trusting her weight to the wall that she built herself, letting her face catch the sunshine. 'I cried like a dog and I was marked for weeks. But the marks didn't last,' she says, and she laughs, her face creasing up, her eyes disappearing. 'Magic skin, remember?' she says, and she tries to hug me. I shrug her off.

Mum would have loved the garden out here at Mountain View. In the end, when the heat kicked in, despite her careful ministrations, only the hardiest, ugliest things survived in her backyard: a scrubby little wormwood and some pale green cacti that never flowered. But she kept at it. My mother's kindness, the softness that I used to hate, that I used to think invited cruelty; it really was something. In all my life, she never was mean-spirited.

I select a couple of the gardening books and take them over to the sofa. The pages are crinkled with water and sun, and bear annotations in her careful hand from what now seems like eons ago. 'Back pot – mist foliage' 'Front of border, cut back in winter' 'Try on trellis?' I leaf through, trying to find the little pink snowflake-flower, but I can't get comfy. Every time I sit down, the weight in my stomach shifts and seems to press against something new inside me. Plus, something weird is happening with my feet today. They've swollen up and the flesh on top looks like it's separating away from the bone: under the stretched skin, there's a layer of something rising up, like cream at the top of milk. It's fluid, of course, I can feel it as I walk, a kind of sloshing around inside my own skin as though I'm wearing water-logged boots. I try to arrange cushions on the sofa so that I can elevate my feet but, as I lean back, the weight of the baby pushes up against my lungs, and I then I feel like I'm choking. I'm no gardener; I don't have the patience or the optimism. By the time I've leafed through the first book properly, finding no sign of that little bugger of a flower, I'm almost looking forward to the barbie.

I take a shower and try to enjoy getting ready, like I used to. I listen to tinny music from my laptop, curl my hair under my chin, paint my face with organic blush and a tangerine-coloured, protected lipstick. When I was younger, I used to get such a brilliant feeling before a big night out in the city. I wasn't always this dour. 'A catastrophist,' Pete says, 'you've turned into a catastrophist, babe, but I still love ya.' There was a time, when I first left home and started exploring the world, when I knew how to enjoy myself. Back at college, we'd do shots in my digs to get things started, excitement fluttering in our bellies, anticipating the heat of the dance floor, the shouted conversations with strangers, the instant camaraderie struck-up in washroom queues, the friends of friends who'd be like family by the end of the night, the after-parties, the intimate confessions, the madcap excursions to the beach and the numb, blissed-out kissing in the cold sand, the insane drives to the edges of the city, to scrubland, to derelict factories, where we'd dance to car stereos and then peel off in twos and threes, holding hands, starting to run, rushing into one another, fingers, tongues, broken glass, amphetamine flutter, pooling, pleading eyes, 'Can, can I just...' Every big night started with that feeling, that feeling that the night was opening up, expanding away from you like accelerating matter, and you were tumbling into a widening darkness; the feeling that the world was getting bigger, that tomorrow there would be new things in it, new people and places, new marks on your skin, new places inside you that ached from laughter and falling on your knees and hooking-up. There was a time when I loved that feeling: in fact, there was a time when I used to think it was the most important feeling of all – to want the world to be bigger, to learn not to be afraid of it.

But that was a long time ago. Before the world started to contract, and everything became more dense and started hurtling back towards me. Before Pete broke me up, before people started to seal themselves in, and before this dead weight in my stomach. Right on cue, my bump palpitates, a painful jab in the ribs, and Pete calls up to me, 'Nearly ready, babe?'

We drive through Lakoomba and I try to relax, but I can't help scanning the streets, searching for anything amiss – a strange expression on someone's face, a clear sign of something being wrong. It's quiet. There's hardly anyone about even though it's Saturday night, but there are no obvious clues of anything untoward. Paulie and Mara's place is right across on the other side of town, at the edge of a dilapidated, redbrick estate. We park-up on the street. Pete carries two large packs of beer down the street and I've stashed a couple of bottles of protected apple juice in my bag. The party's in the backyard: we can hear it a little way off and I can already smell the sizzling meat. I try, for Pete's sake, to make my face look more enthusiastic than I feel. Pete grins at me when we get to number 24, excited to be out, already enjoying the music. He hammers on the front door and it takes a while for anyone to hear us. When the door opens, it's the other guy we met in the bar. He's unshaven and he's wearing a t-shirt that says 'Choke Hazard' in yellow lettering, with an arrow pointing down to his crotch. He grins, widens his arms.

'Pete, good to see you mate. And this is your wife, Alice, right, the fire-cracker?'

'We're not married,' I say. Pete winces; it's almost imperceptible, a tiny tightening through his stomach. I notice it though and I feel like a dick.

'Good as,' Pete says, and puts his arm around me.

'Seems like some bugger needs to make a proposal,' the bloke says, elbowing Pete and jostling him into the house. Pete laughs, and we follow him through a small living-room – empty cans on a low table, tobacco spilled across the carpet, abandoned games consoles – and into the kitchen.

'Help yourselves to anything in here,' the bloke says, ticking his head towards a large table loaded with plastic bottles and tinnies. An untouched chocolate gateau sits at the head of the table, glossing like fresh excrement in the heat. 'We're all set up out here.'

We head out the backdoor and onto a verandah. The garden sinks away 20 feet below us. It's surprisingly lush out here: there's a long backyard, a good bit of lawn, and beyond that there's the start of wild land – a parched, yellow bit of scrub leading towards a swathe of silver eucalypt. I linger on the step for a moment: the trees are moving ever so slightly, the pale leaves lifting as though they're riding a thermal. Behind the eucalypt, a darker section of the forest cuts up dramatically: the beginning of the mountain crags.

Pete is already down there in the fray, greeting people, clapping Paulie on the back. Paulie's mauling the peak of his cap: he catches it between his thumb and the rest of his fist, lifting it off his head then settling it back down, lifting it up and settling it back down, again and again in quick succession. The gesture seems compulsive and vaguely rabid.

'Alice, babe,' Pete calls. 'What you doing up there? Come and say hello.'

Paulie squints up at me. 'How ya going, Alice,' he says, 'come and get some food in that belly.' He claps Pete on the back and guffaws, congratulating him on the magnitude of my stomach, I guess. I must look even bigger from below.

Paulie seems to be in charge of the barbie. When I get down to him, he introduces me and Pete to some of the guys who are sitting around. There's a sharp-eyed bloke called Jonny who nods a curt hello from his deckchair. There's a bloke in a retro suit who gets up to shake our hands. 'Nice to meet you both,' he says. 'I hear you've moved from the city? To this backwater? What the fuck is wrong with you?' He looks from me to Pete and smiles broadly, evidently waiting for an answer. 'So, seri'sly, why'd you do it?'

'Ignore him,' Paulie says. There's a girl in the corner of the garden turning mal-coordinated circles to the music. 'That's Vicky,' he says. 'She's a right laugh when she's less fucked. Best leave her be just now.' There are several other people sitting around, smoking spliffs and flicking ash onto the grass. I can smell the weed burning, I can taste it even: earthy and synthetic at once, dirty and greenly clean. I must be breathing it in, I can't not be. I shut my mouth and try to breathe through my nose. My hand flickers towards my bag – if I put my face-mask on Pete will go ape. Paulie turns back to the barbie, which is smoking blackly. The whole thing stinks of burning toxins. The charcoal for one thing is giving off poisonous fumes: carbon monoxide. It's a little-known method of suicide, burning charcoal in a confined space. What a bloody national irony it would be if we were all painlessly barbequed to death in this garden. And the smoke's just the start of it: I can see a black crust forming on the unprotected meat. Hydrocarbons, totally fucking poisonous. Paulie grips some sangers in his tongs, turns them over, and fat drips through the grill, making the flames spurt up around the diabolical tucker.

'Smells delicious,' Pete says.

'We've got chooks, we've got shrimp, we've got grouper, we've got steak,' Paulie says, 'hope you're both hungry.'

I've got to get away from the smoke and the chemicals. I turn back towards the house, covering my mouth and nose.

'You ok, darl?' Paulie says, leering again. 'Mara was like this too, queasy with food. You'll be fine once you get something in ya.' His laugh is like a grim little cough. 'There she is.' He gestures with the tongs. 'Mara,' he yells, then he wolf whistles. 'Get your sexy fat arse up here.'

Mara is at the bottom of the garden, cradling Iluka. She lifts her face away from the child and towards us: she shakes her head at Paulie, gives him the finger, then waves at us. She turns back to the child, pointing at us and trying to get him to wave too. He just stares up at her, open-mouthed and filthy-cheeked. We all stand and watch her as she walks up the garden, slowly, murmuring to the baby the whole time. The child is beginning to giggle into her face. Whatever she's saying, it's working.

'Give me a hand with this then, mate,' Paulie says, chucking Pete a packet of grey burgers.

'Alright there,' Mara says, to me.

'Alright,' I say. I'm still trying to avoid the smoke, turning away as I speak and cupping my hand over my mouth. I guess I must look awkward, because she stares at me intently, as though she's searching my face for illegible pain, working out what's not being said. I guess that's how you must have to read babies, when they're dumb and suffering. She must be well practised at it.

'Is the barbie bothering you?' she says. 'I remember what it feels like at this stage,' she says, just like she did when we first met. And again, she doesn't elaborate. Is it this choking feeling that she remembers from being pregnant? The feeling that the world is full of dangerous things that might at any moment suffocate you? Or the physical sensation of being pushed around from the inside, every bit of your body newly tender and terrible? The feeling of a fist in your rectum, a foot against your bladder? Just this afternoon, I saw something new rise up under the skin – not the baby, no, it was worse than that. It was some strange triangular edge of my uterus flexing, when I tried to get up off the couch. A fin of cartilage under my own skin, hiding there, prehistoric, inside me. Is it this feeling she remembers, of being terrified of her body, of what it might be about to do, of what it has already done? Or is she remembering the best time of her bloody life?

'Shall we take a walk?' she says. She pushes her mouth against the baby's ear, whispers something to him, and then hands him to Pete. 'You take care of him,' she says. 'It'll be good practice.' Pete grins and the baby starts to cry.

'Let me show you the views from the edge of the yard.' Mara loops her arm through mine. 'Let's get a break from all this.'

When we get to the end of the lawn, Mara pushes against a place in the fence and two planks lift up. 'We just need to squeeze through here,' she says. 'Might be slightly tricky for you, but there's room if you get the angle right. I came down here the day before Lukey was born.'

I push through the gap and follow Mara into the trees. There's a slight breeze out here; it's cooler and the air feels cleaner. I breathe a little easier. We're under the eucalypt now, their silver leaves shivering above us.

'Watch your step,' Mara says.

'So where's the view out here?' I ask.

'You'll see,' she says.

We walk on for a couple of minutes more, until the sounds of the barbie have died back. I'm concentrating on my feet, on not misstepping, on not disturbing a funnel web or a snake or bull ants or any of the other poisonous creatures that might be out here. 'This is the view,' she says. I look up. She's come to a stop at the fringe of the eucalypt and in front of her is the raggedy rock-edge of a sudden drop. We're stood at the edge of a deep ravine, and on the other side, sheering all the way up to the sky, is a vast cliff of jungle green. I have to crane my neck back to see all the way up to the top of it, where the greenery gets sparser and the golden rock breaks through in pointed formations. Even then, there's a tree that grows right out of the top of it, rising from a needle-point of stone.

'Shout,' she says. 'Shout something.'

'What?' I say.

'Shout something!' she says. She cups her mouth and leans towards the ravine. 'Like this. MARA, MARA, MARA.' Her name repeats downwards into the ravine, and I hear the sound fall, ricocheting between the sandy walls, echoing back to us. Mawa, Ma-a, Ma…

'Echo Point,' she says. 'That's what this place is called. Go on. You try it. Shout a name.'

I'm not sure what to shout. I don't want to shout my name: it feels like tempting fate or practising a suicide in sound. My mother's name comes to mind. Is it wrong to shout it? I don't know, and it's all I can think of, so I shout, 'MARGERY, MARGERY, MARGERY.'

Mar-gry, Ma-gy, Ma… the ravine answers, and then swallows the sound. There's nothing after that. Even the trees are quiet.

'Eeerie, but?' Mara says. 'We used to come out here all the time. When we were kids. I can't do it now, not with Iluka. This is going to sound weird, but I can't bring him out here. I love Iluka more than anything else in the world, and I think if I bring him out here I might throw him off the edge, right into Echo Point. Weird, but?' She laughs.

This confession startles me. If I were back in the city, if Mara were a client, I might be duty-bound to call Child Protection about this. Would I have to register concern, initiate some sort of procedure? Mara looks so relaxed about what she's just said. Maybe she's just more honest than other people. Maybe everyone thinks things they shouldn't, wild things like this. Maybe other people are just more secretive about it, more afraid of their own thoughts.

'Have you got a name for the baby yet? Is it Margery?' Mara's settling herself down to sit in the grass right at the edge of the drop; she bends one knee up, angling herself between me and the mountain. I perch on a rock a little way back.

'No, we don't have a name,' I say. 'Margery was my mother's name. She's not around anymore.'

'I'm sorry,' Mara says. She's staring at me intently again, like she's trying to work out if I've got colic or something more serious. I've met other mothers who are intense like this, at pre-natal classes: I guess she might be starved of company, keen to make her ten minutes away from the baby count, wanting to connect with someone who isn't feeding from her. 'I know it's frightening, even more so if your mum's not around. Mine wasn't either. Not really.'

I don't want to talk about my mother, so I don't say anything. Mara carries on.

'The thing is,' Mara says. 'She didn't know how to be a mother. No one taught her. She was half-caste, back when all the Welfare shit was happening. So they stole her away from her mum and gave her to a white family.'

'Shit,' I say. 'That's awful.'

'Yeah,' she says. 'My mother gave me up for adoption, too. Thought she wasn't good enough. Thought I should be with better parents. Gave me away when I was small.'

'Shit,' I say again.

'What about you?' she says. 'Pete's Greek, right? Where are your folks from? I mean, originally.'

'My mum's side were Poms,' I say. 'She moved out here by herself. She didn't talk about home much: said the weather was bad and the people were worse. Said it never felt like home to her anyway, and there was no point dwelling on the past. "Home was where you made your future," she used to say. I never knew her people.'

'What about your dad?' she asks. 'He still around?'

'Italian. Never met him,' I say. 'No idea if he's still around.' I can see she wants to hear more. I remember how this works: trading secrets to forge a friendship. It's been a long time, but I try to remember how to do it. And it feels good to talk, despite myself. 'Turned out he was married when he was with my mum, family of his own. My mum hardly ever talked about him either. She always said I was a windfall. She used to pretend she'd found me under a mulberry tree. She told me the full story eventually, when I was grown. He was a supermarket manager, one of the places she worked. When she got pregnant, he ended the affair. Didn't want anything to do with either of us. Didn't want us disrupting his "family". Apparently we didn't count as family.'

'Shit,' Mara says. 'What is up with that?' She's outraged on my behalf, as I was on hers. I get a little rush of good-feeling: the feeling that someone's on my side and I'm on hers.

'Yeah, well, she always said I could find out more about him if I wanted. I never wanted to. She'd tried her best to forget about him, it seemed out of order to ask questions. Plus, he'd left us, so why should I care? She raised me on her own, worked every hour god sent, never tried to get the law involved when she didn't get her Child Support. Why would I want to chase him?'

'Well,' Mara says, 'the way I see it, we've already fallen lucky.'

'How do you work that out?' I say.

''Cause we both get to keep our babies, and they get to stay with us and their daddies,' she says. 'They get to have a family. Paulie and me, we were both foster kids. I know he seems kind of objectionable. That's just his defence mechanisms. He hates all the polite, nicey-nicey bullshit. We've both met so many softly-spoken, nicely-dressed cunts. You know what I mean? Paulie doesn't have time for that, wants to tease anything bad out of people from the start. He's got a good heart, my Paulie, and he loves Iluka. I can see Pete's going to be the same.' Mara lies back on the ground, lifts her arms and lays them down in the grass over her head. She closes her eyes. It's like she's never heard of brown snakes or redbacks.

'Yeah,' I say. 'Pete will be brilliant.'

'I tell you something I do miss,' she says. 'Being a responsible mother and all. I miss a smoke.' She sits up again, glances at me; mischievous, almost coquettish. 'Obviously I'd never do this around Iluka.' She's fishing around in the deep pockets of her dress. 'And I hardly ever get a chance these days. Never get a moment to myself. I think we all need to kick back, every once in a while. What do you reckon?'

She's got a small, beaten-up tin in her hands and she uses both thumbs to flip it open. Inside, I recognise the shapes: there's a small cube of resin – dark brown stuff, the texture of tiffin – some loose tobacco, some Rizlas and a lighter. She starts warming up the resin before I've had chance to reply.

'I do know how you feel,' she says, crumbling the stuff between her fingers, though I don't remember saying how I feel. This time she's going to expand on it, on what she remembers of being pregnant, I can see it. She's been building up to it, waiting until she thinks I'm ready. And just the action of working the resin seems to relax her, loosening her into deeper confession. 'I was terrified just before Iluka arrived. You know, Elaine, my foster mum, used to tell me these stories when I was pregnant. I was living with her for a while, before I moved in with Paulie. She told me that there are all kinds of different traditions to mark a birth, you know, in different places in the world? Somewhere, I can't remember where, the pregnant woman digs herself a grave. Can you bloody imagine that? When she told me, I thought it was so, so dark. I said to her, "Why are you telling me that?" And she said, "You'll understand when you've had the baby." And I did. I understood it.' She licks along one side of the Rizla paper, sealing up the little spliff she's made. She starts sparking the end, drawing on it until it catches. 'You've made something new, and it's also the end of something old. It is kind of like dying, that's what she meant, Elaine, my foster mother.' She holds the spliff towards me. 'I'm guessing you won't, but I've heard it doesn't matter what you smoke in the last few weeks,' she says.

'No ta,' I say. We sit quietly for a moment and I watch her enjoying that spliff, really enjoying it. She sips the smoke in and lets it roll out of her nostrils. Then she lies back down in the grass.

'You know what else I miss?' she says. 'I miss flirting with people. You know, when you meet someone at a party, and it's probably not going to go anywhere, but there's still that moment of… will it? Where you both think it might happen? Or at least, you just don't know where the night will take you? Do you know what I mean? You're a bit pissed, maybe a bit stoned, and… I don't know, everything feels like it's alive. All of you, every bit of your body, and everything around you too.'

She looks so guileless, lying there, breathing in the smoke with her eyes closed, her body gently pulsing with pleasure in the grass. So unguarded. I guess she must be a good few years younger than me. 'Yeah,' I say. 'Yeah, I do know what you mean.' Actually, she might be really young, nineteen even. The pleasures of younger people, they've begun to seem sort of innocent to me – even the wildest drinking, and the drugs and the screwing: these kids party with total ferocity, because they're playing at the edge of the world, and they know it. But older people, my parents' generation – the

154

thought of their pleasure is distasteful to me, macabre even. They've ruined the world: thinking of them sipping wine in their living-rooms is like imagining neon gas spreading silently through your house; the thought of them fucking is like finding out about a secret arms-deal.

'Oh,' says Mara, exhaling the sound. 'You'll feel like that again,' she says. 'When the baby's come and you can catch a moment like this.' She doesn't open her eyes, but she smiles and reaches out her free hand. 'Come here,' she says. 'Lie down next to me for a minute.'

I hesitate. I don't want to get close to her smoke or the edge of the ravine; but I don't want to leave her hanging there, arm outstretched, unanswered. I can at least still remember what it felt like to be that open, to be at that age when the world was new enough to be exciting, yet obscure enough not to be terrifying. Or maybe Mara knows plenty about the world, has seen it all already; perhaps she's just precociously fearless.

'Listen,' I say, 'if I lie down there I might never get up again. But I'll come and sit with you.' I try to angle myself away from her smoke and I sit cross-legged next to her, taking her hand. She grips mine tightly, and then she loosens her hold, working her thumb around my knuckles. They make little cracking sounds as she works at them.

'You're really tense,' she says. 'Are you sure you don't want a smoke? You know, my mum, my real mum, smoked

155

pot all the way through her pregnancy. Said it helped with her morning sickness. Then again, my mother isn't the best example to follow.' She starts to giggle; there's a short burst, which quickly subsides, then her body ripples up again. She gasps with laughter and I can't help it, it's totally contagious, I'm not even stoned and I start to laugh a bit too. She squeezes my hand again.

This is how I used to make friends, when I didn't see every person and every place as a contagion to be guarded against. It was these moments that used to be so precious that I'd spend all my time looking forward to weekends and trips and parties. And I feel it again, now, just for a moment: the absence of fear. And then it is like I'm stoned: Mara's hand feels vivid and realer than my own and I close my eyes and I lean back and let my weight go into the ground. Maybe, when the baby comes, maybe there will be more moments like this. Perhaps I'll remember how to be open again; or me and Mara will become friends and she'll teach me.

It takes me a while to realise that Mara isn't laughing any more. I open my eyes and she's curled on her side, watching me. 'There,' she says, 'I knew you'd relax a bit out here.' Her pupils are dilated and there are large, dark blooms expanding on the front of her dress. She strokes one side of my face. 'I've got to go,' she says. 'I need to feed the baby. You've got this joy ahead of you.'

'Right,' I say. 'Give me a minute.' I get on to all fours and she gives me a hand on to my feet.

'Better make sure that dog-end is out,' she says, searching with her foot through the grass and then twisting the sole of her shoe hard against the dead butt. 'They're saying the fires are causing it now,' she says. 'And that the fires are getting closer. Trying to get us to move out to the camps again because of the *outbreak*.'

'What?' I say. 'What outbreak?'

'Oh,' she says. 'You know. The cutis thing. They're saying we're downwind of the fires this year and that might be what's causing it. Listen,' she says, 'you don't need to worry. It rained yesterday and the fires aren't getting anywhere near us. They're just trying to get us to leave again.' She's holding my hand and her face is close to mine, and her eyes look massive and beautiful and totally bloody moronic.

By the time we get back to the yard I can hardly breathe; the whole place is acrid with barbie smoke and skunk, and I'm struggling for air after marching back through the trees. Mara is somewhere behind me: she shouted after me, telling me to calm down, and then I lost her and could only hear her voice mewling in the background. There are more people here now, collecting together in various states of reciprocal intoxication, from the slightly-stoned mumbling groups of men, to reclining couples laid on the lawn coming-up together, to the super-high girls who now sweep around the edges of the party, windmilling their arms. The music is louder too. I weave through the different groups, trying to find Pete. A massive man with cans of beer in both hands blunders into me. 'Christ,' he says, eyeing my belly and recoiling. 'Sorry, I didn't see you there, darl.' I push past him. 'Don't know how I didn't see you,' he shouts after me. 'Size of a bloody yeti.' The smoke has a bluish quality, the same colour as the morning mist around the mountains, and I'm wondering now if that pretty haze isn't only eucalypt oil rising in the air, but the pollution from the fires too. I didn't notice it before, but perhaps there was ash on the air, just like there is now, blue and toxic, and my eyes are watering in the haze and if I don't find Pete, I'm just going to leave and drive as far as I can–

'Alice.' There's a hand on my upper arm, gripping me hard. Paulie steps in front of me, takes hold of my other arm. 'Alice? Mara says you had a total epi out there.' He lets go of my left arm and puts his hand firmly on my chest, forcing my breasts apart. 'Christ, babe, I can feel your heart going like the clappers. You need to calm down. You know, this sort of thing isn't good for you or that baby.' He stares into my eyes, then moves his head side to side like an optician. 'Getting all riled up. You and me are going to take a little walk.' He grips my left arm again and moves me to the edge of the party. 'And you're going to breathe with me, you hear me? In breath, out breath, in breath, out breath. You feel this.' He takes my hand and puts it across his mouth, so that I'm walking with my hand across his muzzle like a face-hugger. 'You feel me breathing? In and out? You're going to match it. You're panicking, you're having a panic attack, that's all.' I can feel his breath, hot and damp, across my palm and fingers. I try to do as he says, I try to steady my breath, just so I can get away from him. In breath, out breath, in breath, out breath. We walk like this for several minutes, and no one seems to bat an eyelid. Maybe they think we're dancing. 'That's it,' he says. 'That's it. Good girl.' As though I'm a horse. As though I'm a skittish filly that he wants to keep calm before shooting.

'Where's Pete?' I say. 'Where is he?'

'Now don't get yourself upset again, darl.' Paulie's words are wet on my fingers. 'Pete's over there having a dance. I'll get him once you've calmed down. He's having a nice time, your old man. First time he's kicked back in a while, by the sound of it, and might be the last time he can for a while, after this little one comes. So you don't want to go spoiling it, do you? We're all having a nice time, aren't we?'

We're still walking along the perimeter of the party in this demented fashion: him gripping me hard by the arm, me with my hand held over his face. I cast around for Pete and then I spot him: his back's turned to me and he's dancing with

159

his arms in the air. His body has gone all slack and it looks as though he's being dangled from his hands, like a puppet.

This means he's totally smashed.

'What have you given him?' I say. 'What have you given Pete?'

'Listen,' Paulie says, and now he grabs me hard by both arms and turns me into his body, so his lips are right next to my ear, 'You come over to my house with a face like a smacked arse, you upset Mara, and now you're trying to ruin Pete's night too. You need to chill the fuck out, Alice.' He lets go of me and I stumble backwards. I turn around and scan for Pete again. I'm not going to make a scene. I am not going to let Paulie think I'm hysterical. But we're leaving as soon as possible.

When I get to him, Pete has his eyes closed and his head is dangling backwards. His arms are straight up, grabbing at imaginary ropes in time to the music. I get close to him. 'Pete,' I say. I have to say his name a few times to get him back to earth.

'Ali!' he shouts. 'Babe! I love this tune! Come dance with me.' He puts his arm around my shoulders, tries to shuffle me into dancing. I can see that he's chewing at the inside of his mouth, biting down on his own flesh as he comes-up. Soon his cheeks will be puffed out and he'll have that weird, juniper smell on his skin; his skin will be wet with sweat and chemicals.

'Pete,' I say, taking hold of his hands and lowering them. 'I need to go home. We need to leave.'

'Nah, babe,' he says. 'Everything's just starting. We don't want to go now. It's way early.' His eyes are big and shiny and he stares at me blissfully, then grins and shakes free, nodding his head, putting his arms up in the air again.

I put both my hands on his shoulders and speak directly into his ear. 'Pete,' I say, 'I need to leave. Look at me. I can't be partying. This wasn't part of the deal. If you want to stay then I'll drive home and you can make your own way back. I've got to get out of here. We've got to get out of this place.'

'What are you saying, Ali? I can't hear you!' He's shaking his head from side to side now, like a dog with a tick in its ear. 'Babe, speak up.'

'Pete!' Someone else is calling now, far louder than me. 'Pete, mate.' It's Mara. She comes up dancing behind Pete, with Iluka on her hip. 'Pete, Alice isn't feeling well,' she shouts. 'You need to take her home.'

'Oh!' Pete shouts back in surprise, nodding at Mara and then turning to me. 'Why didn't you say, babe? Poor Alice.' He takes my face in both of his hands, moves the flesh on my cheeks in circles. 'Poor baby. Let's go now. We'll go home and I'll take care of poorly Ali.'

Mara nods at me. 'I'm sorry I upset you,' she says. 'Listen, I'll call in, right? Tomorrow? Make sure you're doing ok?'

'Yeah,' I say. 'Sure. That would be nice.' But what I'm thinking is: I'll be gone, I'll be bloody out of here, I'll be somewhere safe, far, far away from this.

As I drive us back towards the house, Pete drums on the dashboard with his fingers and trills a tune between his lips that is totally unrecognisable.

'Pete,' I say. 'It's pretty hard to concentrate on the road while you're doing that.'

It's getting dark now and the streets are deserted. There are a few lights flickering on people's porches, but most of the houses are the same smoky dark grey as the sky: they have a recently extinguished look, like blown-out candles. Maybe people are leaving already.

'Sorry, babe,' says Pete, and he sits on his hands, trying to keep still even though I can see the urge to dance twitching through his body. 'And I'm sorry you're not feeling well, Ali. Why didn't you tell me?'

'I'm fine,' I say. 'We just needed to get out of there.'

'What do you mean?' he says.

'Mara told me that something is going on. In town. There's an outbreak, I'm sure of it. We've got to leave straight away.'

'What are you talking about, babe?' he says. 'Are you getting carried away again?'

'Listen,' I say, 'Mara said it. She said there's been an outbreak. She used that word, it's not me making it up. She said that the smoke from the fires might be causing it.'

'Well,' says Pete. 'I don't see Mara and Paulie leaving. And where will we go? Back to the city? Which you said was toxic and dangerous? Where we don't have anywhere to live? Or to one of the camps, which you say are hell on earth? Or into the bush, where there's no medical help? You want to give birth in a car, is that what you're saying, Ali? Honestly, it's getting funny now. There's no point pretending to talk seriously when you're like this, babe.' He laughs. He laughs and starts drumming on the dash again.

'Look, I haven't worked everything out yet, but it's not safe here,' I say. 'I want you to ring your mum. Ring your mum and ask her what the news is saying. Ask her if we can move in with her for a bit, just until we've worked things out.'

He snorts. 'You want me to ring my mum now, late at night, to ask if we can live with her, just after we've left? That's insane, Ali. We've got a sweet life worked out here. We planned all this – this is what you wanted, too. I tell you what, if you still feel worried in the morning, I'll drive into town and we can check on the news. I'll go back to the surgery, see what the deal is. We'll get some information, right? We won't go hysterical after a bit of hearsay, ok?'

He's trilling and tapping away again. I can see that I'm not going to get anywhere tonight. Pete's even more blissed out than usual, and it would be impossible to get him to pack-up in his current condition anyway. I briefly calculate the plausibility of leaving him; I could let him fall asleep, pack-up a few essentials, set off in the car back to the city. I'd be there by tomorrow. But he's right: where would I go? Mum's flat has new tenants in it, a family of five. In my condition I can barely fit on the backseat of the car, let alone sleep in there. And I won't be alone, for long, will I? Which of the friends that I've so assiduously frozen out for the last year will want me and a screaming baby on their couch?

'You promise?' I say. 'You promise that first thing in the morning we'll go into town and find out what's going on? And then we'll figure out how to leave?'

'I promise, babe,' he says, 'I do solemnly swear that we'll investigate things tomorrow, find out what's going on and then discuss the situation. *If* you even want me to go in the morning. Things will look different then, after a good night's sleep, I promise, babe.' He stares out of the window, blowing air through his lips and making a ridiculous song.

In bed, swallowed up by the dark, I try to lie really still and I listen for signs of what's really going on. I listen to the noises outside the house, as though the birds and the beasts will speak to me, as though they might pass on some sort of message. I hear a skirmish close by: possums, maybe, wailing at one another, then hissing like cats. Perhaps what happened to the bird is happening to them? What if there are possums out there, sealing over right now, running into one another in fear and blind confusion? I get out of bed, stand in front of the window, try to see if I can make anything out. It's a clear night and in the moonlight I can see the silhouettes of the low, scratchy bushes at the edge of the garden, and then the start of the rustling crop of jarrah: *Mountain Devil*, I hear my mother's voice say, *Old Man Banksia, Waratah*. A dull, deep pain forks through my lower back and down into my pelvis. It makes me bend and grip the edge of the window. It's harder than the kicks usually are; perhaps it's hit my sciatic nerve. The pain's gone as suddenly as it came. I straighten up again, resume my position surveying the garden. There's no sign of the animals. Everything is quiet now except for the rustling trees. And then there's a low, distant, growling sound. The cooling off of hostilities. Perhaps it was just cats after all.

'Babe,' Pete's voice trawls through the dark. 'Come back to bed.'

I sigh, turning away from the window. When I get back into bed I can feel that Pete's body is still restless. We played music out on the verandah for a while, when we first got home. I thought Pete might have danced the drugs off. He curls around me now, starts kissing my neck, his nose and his mouth wet and warm. He pushes one hand into my hair. 'Alice,' he says, softly. His other hand moves across my bump, searches across this vast place for other parts of me.

I turn on to my side, facing away from him. I catch his hand, hold it fast. I push my face against the pillow. It's not just that it would be logistically difficult: the thought of it, the thought of us fucking, makes me want to shrink to nothing. I curl around my bump, hugging myself tight.

'It's ok, babe,' he says. 'I understand.' He kisses my ear. 'Do you remember that first time, Ali? The very first time we were together? At Dougie's house?'

I close my eyes. Of course I remember. We were just sixteen. We were at a party, a house party thrown by one of Pete's friends whose parents lived down by the harbour, a tiny white house in the shadow of the bridge. Most people had gone home or passed out; it was early morning and there were already streaks of pink across the horizon, the next day beginning to spread fire into the night sky. Pete had led me into Dougie's bedroom and we'd fallen onto his bed, kissing, jittery with alcohol and sleeplessness and nerves, our lips sugary and metallic, the blood close to the surface. It had been such a surprise, what our bodies did, their strange intelligence, the way they accommodated one another. We'd curled up in spoons and listened to the gulls cawing over the harbour in the hours afterwards, and Pete had kissed my fingers over and over again as we drifted in and out of sleep.

'I remember,' I say, and I hold Pete's hand.

'I'll always remember,' Pete says. 'And the time we made this.' He scoops both our hands under my bump, so that he's cradling my stomach, warm and fluid, and somewhere deep inside this fleshy, liquid mesh, he must be cradling the baby too.

And when he says that, when he makes me remember that time, I feel like I'm falling, tumbling over the edge of Echo Point with my mother's name. I grip Pete's hand hard. Why did I shout her name? Why did I make her disappear all over again? That night, the night we made the baby, that was the worst. It makes me feel sick to think of it, it makes me hate him. 'Why would you bring that up?' I say. 'Why would you want me to remember that?'

'Because we made something beautiful, from out of all of... that.'

But it was not beautiful. Nothing about that time was beautiful.

My mother had gone into a care home. It's what she wanted, that's what I kept telling myself at the time. My mother was what they politely called a 'geriatric mother': she was forty-two when she had me, and her body was beaten-up by a succession of hard, repetitive jobs: kitchen work, cleaning work, packaging work. She'd had to stop working, by the time I moved out, and her arthritis got bad sometimes, so bad that she couldn't do her buttons up or take care of herself. She began to stay at a place that provided remedial care when it flared up. A care home called 'Sunnyside Up'. She'd been in several times before; it was only ever for a few days, to tide her over when the pain was at its worst. I'd offered to help, to go over before work to get her dressed, but she didn't want me to, said she liked the home and they could give her the proper stuff too, the real pain-relief drugs.

I got the call at work. The voice was familiar: a plump woman with an exhausted manner who I'd met at reception several times when visiting my mother. Her tone was resigned: what she was telling me was entirely ordinary to her, so much so that I had to ask her to repeat it several times, until I understood the words, the importance of them, despite the mundane delivery. My mother had died early this morning. She'd been taken to the hospital but was pronounced dead on arrival. They were very sorry. My mother was a very sweet woman. She'd be missed.

'What?' I said. 'She only had the pain in her hands and her hips. There must be a mistake. There's been some kind of mistake.'

I stared at my office telephone after the woman had hung up, eyeballing the plastic receiver that lay in my hand. How could this dumb object have spoken my mother's death? Ten minutes ago I was sitting here eating cereal and my mother was alive and pretty much well, doing the crossword or chatting with her friends in the home, taking a walk in the gardens, reading and cracking her knuckles. And now this piece of plastic had made her dead. I glanced at the other objects in front of me, which were illuminated in the morning sunshine: the slow drift of tiny specks circulating through the air; the dusky surface of my laminate desk, scuffed through use; the sellotape dispenser, its reel of tape marked with thumb prints; the screen of my computer, showing now all the human dirt it had caught on its once immaculate surface, its speckles of grease, the dust that had accumulated into sparkling dots of dead skin, the prismatic smudges from human hands. All of these objects, all of these dirty hard plastics, would outlast us, would sit here perfectly still, unflinching, as our deaths were announced. These things had murdered my mother, I felt it even then, even before I knew for sure what had killed her.

Kimmy drove me to the hospital. Everything outside was colour and movement and speed, but no sound. The only sound was my heart, banging to get out, and a high-pitch whine that felt like a dispersal alarm dispensed from inside me. Where was I meant to disperse to?

Pete rang me somewhere along the way. 'Are you ok?' this other phone said, this phone in my hand, in Pete's voice. 'Is there anyone with you, Alice?' We hadn't spoken in a couple of months. His voice was newly careful.

'My boss is with me,' I said. 'Kimmy. She's driving me to the hospital.'

'I'll come,' he said. 'I'll be there.'

People always say that when you see someone dead, they're so much less than they were alive: something fundamental has gone. What people don't say is how much *more* the body becomes, how obese the flesh seems when it's left behind, slackened away from the quick. It was as though my mother's flesh had been poured onto the trolley, it was as though the lithe, quick animal of her had been shot and had fallen into dead weightiness.

The room was brightly lit and I was not alone in it. A nurse hovered behind me, sucking a boiled sweet. The cause of death was a massive heart attack, someone had said to me. It seemed hysterically colloquial in the circumstances, the word *massive*. Bloody ginormous. The body was in a nightdress. The flesh on the upper arms was already changing, a dappled yellow pattern veining its way through the fat, and a waxy sheen making the skin look vivid, in a different way to the truly alive: it looked tacky, like cold butter about to soften. The face was unbearable. The lips had parted and the cheeks were already drawing back towards the table, so that the jaw was exposed, all the tiny teeth set in a terrible grind. I stepped closer to the trolley.

The woman behind me whistled as she sucked her sweet clean away. I reached out to touch the body. It would be cold, I knew it would be cold. My hand murmured above the dead hand and, glancing back towards the face, that was when I saw it: I saw that the eyes were not at all as they had been, that the eyes were quite, quite wrong. 'It's not her.' I turned to the nurse behind me. 'It's not her,' I said. 'Margery Ford?' the nurse asked. Her frown gave me hope. Clearly mistakes were made; she was checking the papers held in a clipboard at the foot of the bed. 'Margery Ford, died 01.07, Sunnyside Up Care Home, following 22 minutes of defibrillation.'

'My mother is Margery Ford,' I said. 'But this isn't her.'

I moved to the head of the trolley. These eyes were not at all like my mother's. There were folds of skin around these eyes, which pooled now in tiered mounds. It was as though each eye was covered with stones of flesh. These must have been enormously puffy eyes, completely different from my mothers.

'I think you're in shock, darl,' the nurse said. 'Folk often look different, deceased. It says here, "Possibility of secondary cutis, question mark?" That's maybe why the eyes look different?'

I plunged into her face then. I pushed into her eyes with my fingers, trying to dig back the skin, to see if it really was her, to see if her blue-grey irises were there, glittering under this great weight of flesh. The skin was cold and hard and would not give. I fingered through it, greasily, and there was no way in, no hidden aperture. The eyes were entirely sealed. The nurse caught hold of me, pulling me back.

'She's blind,' I said, 'she's blind. She can't see a bloody thing.' And then I knew what must have happened: I knew that she had woken in the night and could not see. I knew that she had torn at her eyes and found only skin. I knew that she had called out and that I had not been there to hear. And I knew that she had died alone, her heart pumping in deadly, blind fear.

The night after the funeral I slept at Pete's mum's house, in Pete's old room. He'd been beside me all day, not touching me but always staying close. I'd been crying; I'd cried from the moment I woke up, all day long, silently and without much feeling. When people tried to console me, I mumbled incoherently. No one wanted to listen, so I stopped saying it clearly. I murmured it to myself over and over. *She shouldn't have died, she shouldn't have died.* It wasn't a heart attack that killed her, or at least only obliquely: she was sealed in. It should have been recorded: primary cause of death, cutis. It was her own skin that had killed her, it was everything around us and everything we touched and all the poison that even now laced our fingertips and our lips, that travelled into us, deep into our stomachs and our bowels, where it did its obscene work, getting inside our cells, making them go mad, making our skin proliferate, and even now I could see it working anew, the trail of death from Uncle Mike's cigarette smoke, Uncle Mike who was not a real uncle but a man who had toyed with my mother for years, the way his smoke frilled across the warm air at the edge of the party trying to work its way towards me, and the cheap margarine on the egg sandwiches, half-an-inch of deadly yellow hydrocarbon desperate to slick-up my gullet, and the cling-film over the crisps, Jesus wept, who uses cling-film nowadays? with all its lively little poisons clinging to our food, dying to get inside us, to ingratiate themselves into our oesophagi, into our deepest viscera. No one would listen to this, to what I was saying, under my breath. They patted my upper arm, or hugged me close and made shushing sounds. The hospital had refused to listen too, and the Coroner's Office: they would not change the cause of death and had declined to conduct a new post-mortem. The tests for a heart attack had been conclusive. Later in the day, I lay exhausted on Pete's old bed and my face felt bruised and swollen, like rotting fruit. And I was drunk. What else is there to do after a funeral? We'd sat around Pete's kitchen table and his father had brought out the ouzo. We played cards, and Pete's little brother, Harris, looked away every time he caught my eye, pushing his thumbs hard into his eye-sockets, then saying, 'Ali, I can't bear it, I'm so sad for you,' lumbering over and grabbing me drunkenly. Pete had slapped him on the head then, told him not to be a fucking goose. Told him that I'd be fine, that *he* was the one who should stop being such a prissy cunt. And then Pete's mother had batted Pete around the head 'for language', and we drank more ouzo, and their kitchen was full of noise and light, but I knew, as I turned over my cards, thrum, thrum, thrum, thrum, thrum, down onto the table, I knew what was next door: nothing. Full house! But I knew that it was empty, that next door my mother's rooms were quiet, barely hearing us. That we were just an echo in them. That her clothes were folded on her bed, everything turning blue as the sun set, the air setting into stillness. That the flat was sealing itself into darkness. Was it something in there that had caused it, something in her carpets or the curtains, the old mothballs in her wardrobe, some ancient powder she used to scrub the bath? Was it something at the care home, an air-freshener or old lead pipes or asbestos in the walls? Was it something in the ground, seeping in from the derelict factories at our end of town, soaking up into our water and into our food? Or was it something we were breathing right now, some chemical drifting on the night air from the soft-drink plant at the edge of our neighbourhood, sugar and poison on the breeze? I turned my cards over and then tried to leave. Pete's mum held me fast, said I must stay at least tonight, that I was to sleep here, that she wouldn't let me go.

So Pete kept a vigil, lying beside me, still and unspeaking. Until I couldn't take it any more, thinking of our old flat next door, wondering what had happened; until I thought I could taste the poison on my tongue and my breathing was accelerating and I could feel my heart fluttering to get out, as though it knew, as though it knew that it was being imprisoned; until I scratched at my eyes and my ears and my mouth, desperately checking, clawing to unseal myself; until I turned over and bit Pete's neck hard, and told him to fuck me, fuck me, open me back up, don't let me seal up, don't let me, don't let me close off entirely, fuck me, Pete, now, now, no time for protection.

That was it. That was our beautiful conception.

'Ali?' Pete says again, hugging my bump harder. 'In the middle of all that sadness, we made this. I know it's hard, I know it's a sad memory, but it's happy too because of this. You've given me all my best memories,' he says. 'You've given me everything that's precious.'

'You're high,' I say.

'Yeah,' he says. 'But that doesn't mean it's not true.'

We lie still for a while and I try to quieten the energy in my body: that desire to run, the flickering feeling through my legs and abdomen. My stomach feels strange; the lower curve of my belly is hardening. The baby must be turning, pushing itself against me in new contortions.

'Let's try to sleep,' I say. 'We've got lots to do in the morning.'

Pete frets for a while, chewing his cheeks, tiny spasms in his muscles. Eventually he stills. I list things in my head: what we'll take, what we'll pack. It will have to be the bare essentials, none of the baby things will fit in the car; we'll pack two cases of clothes, my mother's books, we'll load it all in the back seat of the car, and then we'll flit. Tomorrow night we'll be somewhere else, somewhere safe from harm.

VII

I DREAM that I'm a light-switch: someone has pulled on my spinal cord, and everything inside me wrenches downwards, a hot white light blistering back up through my body. I dream that a doctor's fist is thrust up inside me, up past the wrist, mauling all of my secret places, trying to scoop my insides out. I gasp awake. My mouth is dry. It's a dream. It's just a dream. But then the pain comes on for real: a hard pulse through my spine. It's early morning, there's only the faintest light at the window. The pain pulls harder, and inside of me everything twists downwards. The pain is in my bones now; it feels like they're trying to twist themselves free. The feeling is so sharp I think I'm going to be sick. I gasp again and stumble up from the bed. My legs are somebody else's legs. I lean back, trying to balance, the wooden floor seeming to shift under my feet. I blink and look down again: a wad of thick, fleshy tissue, whitish and tinged with pink, gutters down between my legs. It splashes onto the floor, like a strange, glowing sea-creature hauled from the dark. I reach a hand behind me – the bed is wet. It's a trick of the light I think, for a moment; it must be the sunrise that's making everything strange, an early-hours hallucination that's made this weird creature of blood and golden-jelly appear as if from me. I stare again at the window: the sun's up and the light is thin and white and realist. I remember a phrase, one of those peppy birthing descriptions they throw around in antenatal classes: 'the show'. Which means the start of things, the plug that has kept the baby sealed coming away from inside. 'The show' sounds so much cleaner, so much more auspicious than this darkly gleaming thing in front of me.

'Pete,' I say. It comes out as a whisper, less than that even. It comes out as a catch in my breath. 'Pete.' I fold back into the bed, I curl myself as tight as I can around my stomach. The liquid on my legs is already cooling. Perhaps it will dry to nothing. Perhaps it will dry and flake off and I will forget all about the showing show, and I will stand up perfectly straight and the ground will stay steady as we pack-up our things and set out in the car and drive for hours and hours until we're somewhere safe and clean.

When the pain dies back enough that it seems like a dream again, I don't sleep, exactly, but I try to block everything out. I curl in on myself and shut my eyes and make my hands into fists, which I push against my ears. I wriggle down under the doona as far as I can and I try to block out the succession of images that light up inside my eyelids: the squiggled veins, the moving blocks of red light, the black pulse of my heart beating on my retina. And when the pain comes back, real and vivid again, I hum and squeeze my eyes shut, but it will not go away. I have to uncurl and stretch my legs right out and then I arch my back, my body one long spasm. When the pain fades away again, I hug myself tight. There is no comfort now. I know it will return, I know what's coming, and it's so bad that I know that I must be dying. I'm one of those animals that I've watched in the past and done nothing for, the dying elephant I saw once on TV with a jackal snout pushed up through its anus, its entrails pulled out while it watched-on, slowly flapping one ear, or that possum we saw once, my mother and I, driving on the edge of the city late at night, where we'd been I don't now know, and the light picked it up at the edge of the road, one of those roads laid straight on top of the dust, the tarmac edge curling and crumbling into the sand, and at that edge the lights of the car picked up its eyes, green and glinting desperately, and we came to a stop and it didn't move, and then my mother said, 'It's stuck,' and I saw that it was a bushtail and its tail had been flattened into the tarmac, run over by some huge wheel, sticking it to the ground, and that the creature couldn't pull free. It stared at us in horror, or in supplication, frozen still. And then it resumed the frenzied activity that we must have interrupted, it tried to drag itself away from its own mashed body part, a twitching dance back and forth, and we could see that the tail was totally pulverised, flattened to matting and black blood, welded to the tarmac, and the poor critter, in a sudden burst of terror and with a terrible cry, pulled itself off the road, leaving the dead tail behind as it lolloped into the bush. We could still hear it crying. 'That possum's not for long without his tail,' my mother says and starts her engine again. My mother. My mother and her soft, soft skin, her skin that wrapped her into darkness. Alone in the night. In pain, just like this, worse than this. She must have heard her own heart as it sped up, the purple muscle tightening like a fist, punch, punch, punching her to death, just like I can hear mine now, beating inside me, and the other heart, the other heart inside me, low down, beating to get out.

'Ali.' The light is brighter now, a yellow spill outside. 'Alice, what's happening?' Pete has uncovered me. He puts a cool hand on my forehead. 'Christ,' he says, and then draws the cover all the way back, so that my bump and legs are raw in the air. 'Cover me up,' I say. 'Bloody well cover me up.' My voice has come back, I can hear it shouting, and I grab the cover back from him and hide myself under it.

I catch a glimpse of his face, sore and puffy, still tender from last night.

'Babe,' he says. 'I think your waters have gone. Why didn't you wake me?'

'No,' I say. 'It's not that. It's too early. And it doesn't feel right. It's something else, something worse.'

'Ali!' He sounds excited. He's dashing round the room, grabbing things. I hear him knocking things out of the way and slamming drawers shut. And then the pain starts again and I groan and I claw at the sheets.

'Alice,' he says. 'Are you having contractions?'

'No,' I say. 'It's trying to kill me.'

And Pete laughs, he actually laughs. 'Alice,' he says. 'It's starting! Shitting hell, it's already started. Right, it's ok, but. I'm just going to need to leave, just for a couple of minutes. I'm going to go down the road to that old coot's house to phone the hospital. Ask them what we need to do. I'll only be gone a few minutes. You hear me, Alice?'

'Yeah,' I shout. 'Bugger off.' And I push my face into the pillow and the pain is so hard I grab at the linen with my teeth and suck the pillow into my mouth.

'Oh, Ali,' he says. 'I bloody love you. It's happening!' And then he's gone. I hear a clatter downstairs and the car start up, and then the sound fades and there's nothing for a few moments, nothing at all: no birds, no possums, no sound of anything moving in the world outside.

* * *

When the pain subsides, I bury myself as deep as I can under the covers, I shut my eyes, I try to hum myself to sleep, but sleep won't come. When the pain returns, I get up on all fours. I grit my teeth and push backwards into it, moving with my bones, following the way my spine seems to twist. It's as though my vertebrae have come alive now, a long snake of bone working its way downwards, pushing to rip itself out through the bottom of my back. As I push back, the eyes in the wooden floor stare up at me, and the sodden creature I produced gleams, and invisible things inside me pulse, organs and bones throbbing to break free. Everything inside and outside of me has come alive, charged with horrible animation. I shout the pain out, I scream it. There's nothing in the background anymore; everything around me is rushing and teeming. And the skin across my belly is crawling with electricity, sharp little currents that dart like eels. I'm inundated; I'm breaking apart.

Where the fuck is Pete? Why isn't he back yet? When the pain fades again, I hang off the side of the bed, and I call out for him. I don't know how long he's been gone. It feels like hours, though it could just be minutes drawn out by the pain. I shout his name again. Of course there's no reply. And then I call out for her: Mum. Ma. Margery. Ma Ma Ma. There's no one to hear me, there's no reply in the house

182

except for the sound of the wooden timbers ticking as they warm up in the morning heat. The eyes in the floorboards have gone back to being knots, the world of things has receded back into the distance again. I cry then, I cry at the sound of my own pitiful voice and the emptiness of the place. My mum used to hum church songs, kneeling at the side of my bed, if I couldn't sleep, or if I was sick or in pain, stroking my hand. She wasn't properly religious, but she'd gone to church school and the songs stuck, she said, and she went to church every so often, even when the promise of redemption began to seem unlikely. *Amazing Grace*, she'd sing into my hair, *how sweet*. I reach out for her now, fool that I am, I search the air for her with my fingers. *Abide with me*, that was another favourite. When I was small I used to turn my face away from her, even as she sang it to me. *Fast falls the eventide*. I'd allow her to comfort me, that was all. I'd allow her to take my clammy hand, but I'd turn my face to the wall. *The darkness deepens*. How much I resented her comfort. How little I gave her, or let her give me, the whole time I was growing up. *Swift to its close ebbs out life's little day*. Thank Christ for Pete. Pete, who let her love him, who danced like a happy dog when she baked him biscuits, who wrapped his arms around her neck when she read to him. Who knew how to be loved and looked her straight in the eye with gratitude. Thank Christ for Pete. *O Thou who changest not, abide with me*.

It's when the pain moves downwards and I start to want to push that I know I have to get out and look for him. I can't stay still anymore, I've got to move. The pressure is low in my abdomen and I can feel it now, the thing inside me, I can feel the whole weight of it pushing to get out. Only it's in the wrong place, it's pushing with its heels against the bottom of my back and it feels like it's going to push right through. The skin across my stomach tingles then numbs, tingles then numbs. I put my hand on my lower belly, then move my fingers downwards against my taut pudendum. It feels strange. The sensation is dull and rubbery. I can *feel* my skin, but I can't feel *my hand* feeling it. It's as though my body is gloved in a soft, dead pelt. I've got to get out of the house. That's all I know: I've got to move. It's a feeling I remember having as a child, when things got bad and I wanted to run them off, rushing head first into the warm wind blowing off the sea. That's what I need to do. I need to move with speed, to throw my body into a hurtling point and plunge through the world. I want to outrun the pain and this thing inside me. I push myself off the bed. I try not to be deterred by the way everything seems skewiff – if I move quickly enough, surely I'll stay upright. It's a drunk's logic and I stumble at the door, but I make it through to the bathroom. I lean on the wash basin and catch my breath; I splash water on my face over and over, and then I pull my hair back in a band. I glance down at my legs: that's too much to deal with. I find a long dress in the wash-basket and pull it on over my head. My body is acting like it's never been dressed before; my limbs are unpredictable and my balance is seriously off. It's like I'm trying to dress a toddler. I laugh. I laugh out loud at my ridiculous body. And I drag the clothes down over my head. I'm dressed and I'm upright and my heart is pounding to run.

When I open the front door the sky is the bluest it's ever been: dazzling, unreal, not a wisp of cloud in it. And it's hot. Seriously hot. I try to run, and stagger instead. I have to rest before I even make it to the road. I lean on the gate post. I gripe, and there's nothing to come. I spit and try to straighten up. Christ, it's hot. But I've got to get down there, I've got to get to the old man's house and see where Pete is. The clock in the living-room said it was past noon, so he's been gone for hours. I still have the urge to run, to move quickly enough to outrun the pain and leave all of this behind. I start a kind of jog, and even that's too much. I pull up and power walk instead, pushing hard through the balls of my feet, holding the weight of my stomach in both hands. When the pain feels like it might be about to come back on, I walk faster. I shout and I curse and I punch my feet into the pavement and I keep on moving as quickly as I can. Over to my left are the mountains, blearing into a massive blue haze on the horizon. The sky around them seems almost to smoke, shading into violet above the peaks.

The green of the distant forest has this smoky filter too, the swathes of eucalypt turning grey-green, grey, and then, furthest off, where the forest curves out of sight, dark blue. There is no wind; nothing moves. Except for my feet, except for my feet pounding down against the earth.

And then there is the sound of something else up ahead. A car, I can hear a car approaching. A rust-coloured car, nosing its way slowly up the hill. It looks like it hasn't been driven in a while. The orange paint-work is patchy, a colour you don't often see, and the engine is making a horrible grinding sound. The woman behind the wheel is drawn up practically to the windscreen: the windows of the car are dirty, furred up with green, but there's one patch that's been wiped clean and she stares out of it, looking left and right, clinging to the steering wheel for dear life. She clocks me up ahead of her, stares at me open-mouthed. I wave. 'Hey,' I shout. 'Hey.' She's still staring at me, though she's not slowing down. As she approaches, she scowls. She winds the window down. 'You need to get help,' she shouts out at me, the car still moving, 'you need to get away from here.' No shit. As I glance through the gap of the window I see that the car's full of her stuff: there's a pet-box covered with a cloth on the passenger seat and an open cosmetics-case is spilling tubes across the foot-well beneath it; the back seats are crammed with bags and small cases, a lamp, a mirror, old photo albums. She's doing a flit. 'Hey, wait up,' I say. 'Why are you leaving?' She's already past me and the filthy window is closed back up, and the car is too far on for me to kick it.

When I get to the old man's house I'm so hot I can barely breathe. My skin is tightening across my shoulders and cheekbones, puckering into pinkness, and the skin across my belly is the worst: tight and hot and desperately itchy, running with horrible flickering pulses like the ticks you get in muscles when you've been running, like the convulsions in metal heating up too quickly. I need to get inside and I need to drink water. I walk down the path and pause in front of the house. The door is ajar, beneath that horrible canopy of webbing. The silk is so thick in places that it looks like white candy-floss. I can see at least two spiders, fat and well-fed, perched in the centres of their webs. 'Alright,' I call out. 'Hello? I'm looking for Pete. Hey, I really need some help out here.'

Nothing. No sign even of that mangy cat. I eyeball the spiders. Come on then, mother fuckers, I'd like to see you try to cocoon *this* beast of a meal. Two for one. I shrug my shoulders up towards my ears, to make my dress touch the back of neck. And then I take a deep breath and step up onto the porch. I rap on the open door. Still nothing. There's that strange smell, much stronger now: metallic and sweet and sceptic. 'Hello,' I shout again, and I hear something move inside – a shuffle and then a low grumble. 'Listen, Mr Prendergast,' I say. I'm trying to muster my no-nonsense demeanour, the one I employ with difficult clients at work: angry young men who don't want to leave their homes, angry old men who don't want to move from their piss-soaked cardboard canopies. I will be clear and firm and give no opportunity for refusal. I will be reasonable and collected, despite the way the world is blurry and my body is trying to break apart and nothing will stay still around or inside me. 'I need to talk to you, mate. I'm not from the authorities, I'm not trying to sell you anything. I need to know if you've seen my boyfriend, Pete. I need to use your phone. And I…' I look down at my stomach. Why is it so hard to say it? My tongue is hot and flabby. 'I… I might be…' I can't say it. I can't say what I might be, what my body might be doing. 'I… I need a drink of water,' I say instead. 'So I'm going to open the door now.'

I wait a while, and when there's still no response, I push the door open, slowly. At first it's difficult to make anything out: the windows all have nets and there's junk everywhere. Unopened mail banked up at the side of the door, rotting shoes in piles, cat shit in several places, now white and desiccated. I've seen this sort of thing before. I cover my mouth and nose with my sleeve. Further back in the house, I can see a kitchenette, a small L-shape of counter-tops, and every surface is covered: pans, bowls, glasses with tide-marks, cartons, tins with their mouths hinged wide open. Something moves, something shifts low down in the kitchen in the midst of all the debris. My first thought is rats – not that this in fact an old man, slumped on the floor, barely distinguishable from the debris around him. I didn't see when we visited before how thin he was: completely emaciated. Six stone at best, I reckon, which is about the point where you'd lose your mind and start hallucinating. Pete was right, he needs help quickly. The old man groans, his head lolling down onto his chest.

I don't want to go further into the house. I know about cat shit and toxoplasmosis. The smell here is super poisonous. I just need to get him to speak to me. 'Alright,' I say, moving my sleeve away from my mouth for just a moment. 'You've got nothing to worry about. I'm not coming near you. I don't want to disturb you at all. I just need to know if my boyfriend, Pete, came here. You remember, we were here a few days ago? I… I'm…' He's lifting his head up now, with some considerable effort. His eyes are dark and I can't read his expression, but he's looking at me. 'I'm pregnant,' I say. 'In fact, I might be in labour.' I feel a great distance from my own voice as I say these words: labour is something that happens to other bodies. Labour is something contained; it's measurable, containable work. It's working hard to produce something. I can surely deal with a labouring woman, I can take the steps that are necessary to take care of her. It's just that it's not really me who's labouring. What's happening to me feels immeasurably deadly, uncontainably destructive. 'This is important, mate. I need to know if Pete used your phone and whether he went into town from here. Did something happen? Did he go down to the Medical Centre?'

The man's still looking at me. His voice is barely audible: a horrible sound cracks out of him. He doesn't make words at first: it's just his gummy mouth, trying to find traction. He gulps a couple of times, and then he spits it out: 'Sorry.' It's the driest, ugliest word I've ever heard.

'You don't need to be sorry,' I say. 'We can help you sort all this out, if you want us to. I just need to know if you've seen Pete.'

The man's head lolls back down onto his chest, but, ever so slowly, he raises his left arm. Scarecrow-like, his hand hangs from his wrist, and he points with a finger over to my right, to the darkest part of the house.

I put my sleeve back over my mouth, press it firmly over my nose, take a step further in. I can still smell it though, the horrible metallic tang, vivid with faeces now as well. There's a living-room area over in the darkness, a rug of some kind that looks thick with filth. There's a couch, an upright museum-piece, and there are two high-backed chairs turned towards it, facing away from me. I take another step in. I'm fighting back a shiver of nausea, but I have to see, I have to look more closely, because there's something in that chair over to the right of me, there's a wisp of white hair above the seat and, as I move towards it, I can see something claw-like – a hand, a set of nails, digging-in, holding hard onto the end of the arm-rest. Christ. Fucking Christ. It's a woman, barely a woman, an emaciated old coot in a dressing gown, hard with rigor mortis, the flesh still on her but wet and red and starting to melt down into the chair, so that you can see the bones in places, the tiny bones of her fingers, braced hard, digging into the chair and, at the end of the fingers, her perfectly lacquered mauve fingernails. My stomach twists but I don't move. Her face is still mostly intact, so she can't be that long dead, not in this heat. Her face is the worst: her eyes are wide open. Her eyeballs haven't yet shrunk, but the vitreous is parching away, making them look like old seafood. She is staring straight ahead, sightless, as if she's watching a bomb-blast on the other side. The tendons in her neck are braced hard and her cheeks are beginning to clot into gore. The middle of her face is unmistakeable: a white, shiny mask sealing up the nose and mouth. I let myself hope, just for a moment, that I might be wrong. That it's the spiders who've done this, those creatures squatting outside, waiting for death; that some funnel-web has filled her in, entered through her nose and made a home in her wet skull. I take a half-step closer, and then there's no mistaking it. The mask is her own: a weird, white, fleshy mesh, perfectly intact. Her lips are sealed, her nose is blocked, the skin is stringy and taut and dead still. Cutis.

I don't scream. I don't make a single sound. I'm not sure I can even move. My breath is high-up in my chest, coming fast and shallow. I turn my head slowly to look towards the old man, so slowly that I feel as if the scene is an old film full of glitches, slowing, stopping, stopping, stuttering. The old man is still there, and he's still pointing. Or the film is stuck, and I'm seeing it again and again – I'm trapped in this moment, his arm still pointing over to the corner of the room, the bones of his hand dancing like a marionette's, only now I see that at the side of him there's a long gun laid on the floor, an old rifle. The tennis racket we thought we saw.

I need to get out of here, I need to get out of here so fast, but I'm locked to the spot and I turn back to the living-room and follow the man's gaze, and his drooping arm. It's then I see the telephone-table. Right at the back of the room, in the corner, an old-fashioned telephone-table with an adjacent seat. And an old telephone sits there, a phone with a circular face, just sitting there, all prim and neat and ready to dial. I could cry at the sight of it. I can call the hospital, and find out what's happened to Pete, and work my way out of here, and get someone to help with all of this.

'I need to use your phone, mate,' I say. 'It's not about your wife. I'm not interested in your wife. It's just, I'm in trouble, and I need to call the hospital.'

'Dead,' the old man says. 'Telephone's bloody dead. Forgot, didn't I? He couldn't have used it anyway. Bloody idiot.' His scarecrow hand slowly and repeatedly hits the side of his own head. 'I forgot.' He starts to moan, an awful, low, keening sound. 'Didn't mean to, I didn't mean to.'

'He? Do you mean Pete? Did Pete try to use the phone?'

'Sorry,' he says, 'Sorry mate.' And he carries on talking, and I can't listen to the words because I'm walking, I'm walking towards the phone, and there, keeled over behind the sofa, is another body.

I laugh. That's what happens next. I hear myself laugh. Bloody Pete, bloody curled up on the floor. I recognise his t-shirt, and the round of his back, and I recognise the warm brown muscles of his calves. The way he's curled over means that I can't see his face. But I can see the soles of his shoes, and the nape of his neck, and the backs of his knees. And all around him is a shimmering pool. The smell is so strong, the smell of fresh blood and fat. The smell of a butcher's shop.

'Pete.' The word comes out as a whisper at first, as shallow as my breath. Then I'm shouting it. 'Pete. Pete, get up, Pete.' I'm round the back of the sofa now, kicking Pete from behind. 'Fucking get up Pete, stop pissing about.' Pete just takes the impact, his head nodding again and again as I kick him. And the pool around him dances and splashes up over my feet, bright, bright red.

And all the time the man is talking at me in the background, chuntering away as though he can't stop, barely sensible, '…and he wouldn't take no for an answer, he wouldn't just go away… and I told him not to come in, I told him me and Susan didn't want disturbing… you can shoot a man if he's in your house… we didn't want disturbing, can't have them interfering, I can't have them trying to take her away again… and he wouldn't stop… after the shot, he went down bloody hard, he really went down… didn't think it'd hit him… I didn't mean to… he went down so bloody hard… and he was still talking, saying "Alice, Alice," over and over, "you've got to help my Alice"…'

I kneel down in the blood and I run my hands through Pete's hair. His scalp is still warm. I can't look at his face.

When the next pain hits, I'm out on the threshold of the man's house. I manage to get myself off his porch and on to the lawn before I vomit. I stay there for a while, on my hands and knees in the long grass, while the pain works through me. I can still hear the man's voice, warbling on. *You can kill a man who comes into your house… I didn't mean to.* Something moves in the long grass close by and I catch the stink of cat piss: yellow eyes gleam at me through the foliage with all the compassion of an alligator. I will not give birth here; I will not die on this lawn and let myself be eaten by his mangy fucking pussycat. I have to move, I have to put everything else out of my mind and focus on moving.

When the pain has passed, I'm back on the road. After that house, after that dark, filthy space, the world feels even bigger and brighter and more horrifying. The sky rises above me, burning blue all the way up to that blistering sun, and beyond that to god knows what, to those impossible, infinite spaces hurtling beyond. I lock my eyes back down to the horizon. But there's nothing comforting there either: the Blue Mountains sprawl ahead of me, further than I can properly imagine, hundreds of thousands of miles of rock and forest and swamp. And seeing the massive outline of the mountains makes me think of how much is below them too: how many miles of compacted dirt and bone and nickel are under my feet before you get to the glittering centre that once burned so hard it convulsed these mountains up and out, birthing them with such force that they stand here still: violent effigies of that first fire. It's hot, it's too hot. There is no air. There is not air enough to make all this breathable. I can feel my lips cracking. But I keep on up towards Mountain View. Everything is behind me now. I know where I need to be. I've got to get myself somewhere small and dark and cool. I need to get back to the house, I need to hide myself away, to fold myself up into the tiniest space I can find. I lurch forwards in this awful stumble-run. I'm moving as best as I can, the weight in my body pulling me forward, making me gallop, then tumble, again and again, almost falling, staggering, my hands grazing the things I stumble against: the sharp edges of old paint, hardened and peeling away from the fence at the side of the road, the tarmac of the pavement as I wheel forwards, almost falling flat on my stomach, coming to rest on my hands and knees, my palms burning. I push myself up. I go again, tumbling at least twice more. No cars pass me now, though two water planes fly overhead, low to the ground, like they do when there are bush fires.

When I get back to the house the front door is wide open. I must have left it this way, demented in my rush to get out. It's obscene, the house hinged-open like this, totally exposed to this vast, teeming, diseased world. I'm inside lickety-split and I slam the door behind me. The living-room is so full of light. It's irradiated in the midday sun, everything white and dead: the beer bottles from last night, Pete's sweater discarded over a chair, his trainers kicked off at the side of the room. We should have gotten blinds. I should have got curtains. I could tape up paper, but the light would still find its way through. I turn around and around in the room. I've got to find a place to hide, a small, dark hole I can disappear into. The strangest thoughts flash through my mind, as brief, mad moments of hope: I think about going up to our bedroom and dragging out our biggest suitcase, curling up inside it, and being zipped in. I imagine waiting until night falls, going out into the yard and digging myself a grave. I'll climb in and splutter out this thing inside me, both of us a secret in the cool, wet darkness, and then I'll cover us over and we'll disappear into the earth. I know these things can't happen. I know I can't dig a hole or contort myself inside a case. It's happening too quickly, it's pushing so hard now, and I can't help but push back, and everything feels like it's about to come apart.

It's then that I remember the small space under the stairs, a tiny dark triangle of a hole that we haven't yet filled with our things. I dart towards it as the pain subsides. There's a naked bulb descending from above, the underside of the stairs making a staggered ceiling like one of those geometrically impossible paintings. It's a space too small for a human body, and it's about to be crammed full of two. I don't try the light switch. I just push myself in, folding my body into the space, my coccyx against the floor, my head jammed against the inverse of a step, my legs pushed upwards against the wall, and I pull the door closed behind me. There's still a tiny crack of light, but the rest of the space is dark enough to dull my vision so that I don't have to see my body. The weight in my stomach has moved: ordinarily I'd be choked in this position, but everything is moving downwards now. I let my head rest against the cool plaster and I groan, long and hard. If I could howl I would: I don't have the energy. I'll take a nap, I think, a tiny little nap, and all of this will fade into dream, and then I'll wake up and the last few hours will melt away and me and Pete will be back in bed together, planning our escape.

I close my eyes and try to blank myself out. In the dark I see the curve of Pete's back on the old man's floor again. Where was the shot? I saw the blood, thin and bright as fine wine, but not the wound. It must have been in his belly, he must have folded himself over the bullet. I should have looked at his face. I should have made sure his eyes were closed. I should have closed them with my fingertips and kissed them, kissed the folds of his eyes like he used to kiss mine, so tender, before we went to sleep. How could I have left him there? Pete would never have left me. He'd have stayed with me, he'd have carried me up the road and kept me close to him. All the times that he's kept me close. Not just after my mother had gone; my whole life, our whole lives, he's kept me so close. We're nine, and I'm going to a new school, and I tell him that I don't like the walk home, that trucks rush past on the main road and the older boys shout things at me. And the next day I see him, a distance off, trailing me the whole way home on his bike. He stays close to me until I tell him to stop, until I tell him it's weird, and he looks hurt and confused. We're fourteen and we've been sent home from school because a storm is coming, a massive storm that has brought flash floods in the north. I'm walking home with friends when the light changes: the sky turns dark and the air makes us suddenly shiver. We pick up our pace, but the sky moves more quickly and, even before the rain hits us, the drains start to gurgle with the water that is coming. We start running, and then somehow Pete is beside me. 'Keep hold of me, Ali,' he says, gripping me hard, 'we need to run faster,' and before I know it we are home and Pete is putting bags of flour against my mother's door and lining the window frames with towels, and he holds our hands as the flood waters surge through the estate, brown and foaming. The water's gone as quickly as it came and it leaves behind a horrible trail of sewage and trash and car parts and street signs. 'No one's going anywhere,' Pete says, proud of himself as our protector. 'Until I've been out and checked we've got the all clear.' We're nineteen and we're camping at the edge of the bush. A place he's been to before, with his brother and father. A place he wants to show me. We hike in the day, and he packs things for us to eat along the way. The heat makes me feel full, so I won't eat the semolina cake his mother has given us. 'You'll get bonk,' he says. 'Like cyclists. Your legs will suddenly give way.' We keep walking until we find a small lake, hidden in a depression at the foot of the mountains. 'This is it,' he says. 'This is the most magical place I've ever been. This is what I wanted you to see.' And he kisses me, shyly, and turns around in the open space, tilting his face up to the sun. The dust underfoot is red; the pool is bright blue and still as glass. Tall orange flowers surround the water, their blooms like orbs of fire. It's strange, this place, but Pete loves it. We sit on rocks and throw pebbles into the lake, which swallows them with barely a ripple. And Pete balls the semolina cake into little patties and feeds them to me as if I'm a tiny chick. That night we curl up in our tent and he talks into my hair, barely audible, when he thinks I'm asleep. 'You're my best thing, Alice,' he says, 'you're my most precious thing.'

There's a new dart of pain, hard and deathly through my pelvis. I gag again and nothing comes up. I'm cold and shivery now and the old sensations are back, the needling across my stomach and down through my pelvis. It's trying to prise me apart, this thing inside me, and I can feel it moving downwards, I can feel the force of it tearing at me.

And suddenly I need to let it out, I need to open my legs and push as hard as I can to get this thing out of me. I've got to get out of the closet. I barge the door open and fall out into the living-room. I pull my knees up to my chest and I start to dig at my own flesh, pulling myself apart. The sensation isn't right; it feels as though I'm touching myself with gloves on. My skin is numb and I can't feel my own hands across my pubis. But I can feel the shape of a head, bulging between my legs, and I cup it in my hands; my hands move across numb flesh, again and again. And again. There's no opening. There's no opening in the skin. I run my fingers back and forth, searching, but I can only find a ridge of skin, rising above the baby's head. Fucking Christ. I crawl to the kitchen, looking for something I can use as a mirror so I can see what's going on, so I can see if this is really happening or if it's some kind of birthing delirium. I've heard that people see things when they're giving birth, that they say strange things, that time loses all meaning. Who's to say I'm not hallucinating?

I've got to check. I stagger upright. There isn't anything I can use in here. I turn around and the light catches on a large mirror hanging back in the living-room. It's not easy to get it down from the wall, but once I have it, I lean it against the boxes in the corner of the room and slowly lower myself in front of it. I take a deep breath. I open my legs and stare hard at my reflection. The woman there is barely recognisable: her hair hangs in damp clumps and her face is flushed, split veins running like red spiders across her cheeks. The rest of her skin looks sallow. Her eyes are dark and sunken; her legs are streaked with gore and her feet are horrible – they're covered in dried blood, the skin stained to leather. I lean in to look at my reflection more closely, to see if what I can feel is true. And, as I search and search, all I can find is skin, new skin, skin meshing into new fabric. And there it is, I can see it in the mirror, a newly-knitted thin white seam between my legs. My fingers scramble at it over and over, looking for a snag or a break. There is none. And it's what I always feared, it's what I tried to outrun but can't:

I'm sealed, I'm sealing up, I'm being wrapped inside myself. I can feel the round weight of the baby's skull pressing into my hand, pushing to come out. And inside, I can feel it pressing on the inside too: a bright burning sensation, the bones of my pelvis pulling apart and being held fast.

I push myself up onto all fours and I cry then, just for a moment, because the pain is so strong that I know the thing inside me must be struggling for life too, struggling against my skin, and that it will fight me to the death, though that would do it no good. I pant for a few seconds until the worst of it has passed, and then I pull myself up onto my feet. What do I do? What do I do? Do I let it just carry on? Do I let my skin seal me and the baby in? Do I lie down and let us both be sealed into a catacomb of my skin? I think of my mother again, alone in the night, fastened into her body, trapped and calling out. No. It's not over. It's not nearly over. I'm going to do something. I'm going to do something to stop it and I'm going to do it fast, before I have a chance to think it through and get too scared.

I search the kitchen shelves for spirits. We've not brought much with us, but there's a bottle of ouzo and a small bottle of vodka. I take a deep glug of the ouzo. It's been months since I've drunk alcohol and it feels like straight-up poison: I'm drinking petroleum straight from a can. I take another big glug. Then I search through the kitchen drawers. I grab three knives: one is our sharpest, a long, clean blade that

Pete uses for slicing meat; then there's a shorter one that I prefer for cutting – more control, and a thinner, slightly blunter blade; and then there's the carving knife, with its long, bright, serrated edge. I take the vodka and I use it to douse the carving knife. Then I run the knife under hot water, just to be sure. It's clean, it's got to be clean now, and it's almost too hot to touch but it's gleaming as though it's clean, so I've got to do it and I've got to do it now, before it's too late.

I fill a bowl with hot water and I grab as many tea-towels as I can find, and by the time the next pain hits I'm back on the floor in the living-room in front of the mirror. I lean back for a moment and moan as the pain tears deep into my rectum. And then I take another glug of ouzo and try to steady my hand. I look at the woman in the mirror, the blood-drenched wraith who's staring back at me with a carving knife in her shaking hand. I watch her position the knife between her legs. I watch her try once and I watch her courage fail: she pulls the knife away at the crucial moment. Then she takes the knife in both hands and tries again. She places it carefully, lining it up vertically with the strange white tissue between her legs. She waits for a moment. And then, as her body buckles with the next gasp of pain, she gulps her breath in and slowly, deliberately, pushes the serrated edge into her flesh. And I feel the pain a long way away. It's a series of tiny, fizzy pin-pricks in calloused skin.

Nothing happens for a moment. I sit there, watching myself sitting perfectly still in the mirror. I turn the knife over in my hands and each scalloped point has a tiny blur of blood on it. I stare at myself again, and now I can see something happening. Little pearls of blood appear along the seam of skin, like little red stones glistening on a string.

I take the knife again. I line it up and press it slowly into myself again, careful not to go too deep. Again, there is barely any feeling, just the distant prickle of something too far away to be real pain. When I move the knife, my body contracts, juddering downwards. So I lean back and push, I push my legs as far apart as I can. I scream downwards. The blood is collecting in little drops and running away from the perforations I've made into the folds of my pelvis. I push and I push and I feel the skin stretch. I'm about to take the knife up again but the pushing won't stop, I'm pushing so hard that my teeth are grinding together, and suddenly everything breaks apart. There's a gush of liquid and blood between my legs, and I can see in the mirror the curve of a dark mound moving towards me, extending from the woman's vulva like an enormous blood clot. I gulp the air, I lift my face upwards and I gulp and I gulp, and I try to stay calm. I take another swig of alcohol and I lean backwards again. Another deep pain, another push, and this time I can feel the skin tear with all the burning pain of a skin that can really feel. I use my hands to hold the head that's emerging from me. I keep on pushing, and then I can feel shoulders, a smooth belly, the hardness of feet, quickly guttering out of me. And then more, more still coming, the cord, and more liquid, more blood, more and more hot blood, spattering out of me so fast. I gasp and gasp and then I gather the skin between my legs into my hands: it's warm and wet, and in places my fingertips meet textures I've never felt before, strange frills of torn, stinging skin around the hard cord. I'm open, my skin is open again.

I lean back on my palms and let my head drop. I breathe deeply and my body begins to slacken. Everything that has been braced so hard is loosening off, collapsing. The skin of my pelvis feels especially strange: prickling with heat. My body feels more distant and more vivid than it ever has; the sensations running across my skin are both blurred and sharpened, the way that sometimes happens after heavy drinking. I can feel my pulse, in my perineum and all the way through the new tears inside me.

Exhaustion washes over me in a great wave. I know I need to look at it all, to take a proper survey. And it occurs to me that there should be crying at this moment, there should be some sort of sound to mark the passage, to show that we are through, that me and this thing I've birthed are through to the other side that is life. If that's where we are. I right myself. I open my eyes and steal myself to look in the mirror: between my legs is a blessed mess, the skin frayed away, the blood still seeping. And then there's the cord, twisting out from deep inside me, purple at its core and coated with a clear film. It extends away from me like a line of something impossible: a line of red, burning sand twisting into glass. I made this, I must have made this, throwing it out, a life-rope of plaited blood, and yet I can feel nothing when I touch it. The bloody fingertip that skirts it is clean and dull by comparison.

At the end of the cord, curled like a weird telephone, is the child. Thing, thing is a better word, a thing, a creature I do not know how to name. It does not move. It lies on the floor like a lozenge, its legs folded up against its body, its head bowed into its chest. It's a pellet of life, deep purple, thickly glossed with yellow and white. It looks larval rather than human, like the egg of a bee, slicked in honey and wax and gore. It does not look like a child. And it does not move.

I feel another pain shudder through my abdomen, an echo of the earlier waves. Something else is moving inside me and, as I arch backwards, another creature slips out of me, whooshing wetly against the floor. It shivers there, bright and red. I can barely look at it, it's so vivid. It's enormous and still palpitating softly at its edges, like a giant, beached blood-jelly. This must be some part of cutis, some new horror to accompany my silent egg. I steal another look: it's shimmering in the light, iridescent and deadly as a boxfish. I've never seen anything so red. And at its centre is a network of capillaries so dense that they're black; the whole creature wobbles, a living disc of blood. It sits there pulsing, red and wet and terrible, and the cord still links it to the other thing. I turn back to the first creature and try to find a face now. Is there anything underneath the fatty white mask? There are eyes, I can just about see them, and the snub of a nose. But the eyes are shut. The baby's eyes. My baby. She. She looks as though she has sealed herself fast against this world, as though she prefers the darkness of the womb and doesn't now want to see. She. Poor little she. Her eyes must be sealed: the waxy skin has closed her face and that livid body of blood at the end of the cord has stolen all of the life from her.

I can feel tears on my face, but my body doesn't move or make a sound. Between my legs is hot and the blood is still coming. I don't know how long I sit like this: it is seconds, perhaps, or minutes. It feels like the world has stopped moving and we are all frozen: me, and her, and the disc of blood. It feels like the elongated moment of a fall, when you wait for the pain to arrive in the long, numb tumble.

There's a noise. A loud noise. It's in the room and it's not coming from me or from the bloody tableau between my legs. There's the noise again, a hard rap. I recognise the sound in a dim way, like remembering a word from a forgotten language. The noise is a knock. There's a knock at the door, again and again, and a voice saying, 'Alright? Alice? Mate? You in there? I need to talk to you.'

A woman stands in the doorway. I've never seen anything so pristine. She stands there surrounded by light, her hair pulled back off her clean, dark face, her body perfectly intact: no wounds, no signs of violence, her skin perfectly in place. She's so clean she seems ethereal, a dream of a body without pain. She's speaking: words issue from her, low and quick. Perhaps she's an angel. I know her, but I can't place her.

'Christ, Alice,' she's saying. She's crouched at my side now. 'Christ.' She glances round at the mess in front of me. Pigs eat their dead young sometimes. I remember my mother telling me that. Maybe it's to hide the shame of letting your child die.

'There are footprints in blood all along the road,' she says. 'Christ Almighty, Alice, what happened?'

She glances round at everything: the knife, the bottle of vodka, the curled red mess on the floor. She stares at me, starting to mouth something, and then she stops, wordless. Mara. Mara and I shouted into Echo Point together, yesterday; was it only yesterday, a day ago, before the world was so bloody? She's still staring at me, and then she does the strangest thing: she takes a towel from my side and gathers the creature up. She rocks the bundle hard against her chest. She rocks and rocks and pats the bundle, and then she peers into the clutch of fabric and rocks some more.

'She's cold,' she says. 'She's cold, the poor thing,' and she sings a song I've never heard and pats the bundle so ferociously that I realise she doesn't understand that the baby is dead. And I feel sad for her, rocking a dead thing like that.

'It's cutis,' I say, and I point towards the enormous clot on the floor. 'It's all gone wrong,' I say.

Mara looks at me and then at the shimmering thing. 'That?' she says. 'That's just your afterbirth, darl.'

There's another noise: a small peal of sound from inside the bundle. Mara hands me the towel, pushing the cloth down and putting the wet little creature against my skin. 'Hold her,' she says. 'She's early, s'all. She's small. She needs to be warm.'

I look down at the face of the creature: it's all creased up and her mouth is a bright, red, soundless O. Her eyes are closed and swollen, and the skin is purple and swollen there, like a blind baby bird's. But her mouth is working, opening and closing, a tiny beak. 'But she's blind,' I say. 'She's sealing over.'

'No,' Mara says. 'You bloody goose. Give her a chance. She's had a surprise and she's only just waking up.'

I gather her hard against me then, and I rock her like Mara did, feeling the throb of her body against my chest. She's hotter than me; I can feel my skin cooling under the layers of blood and sweat. I'm shivering. I'm cold and I'm shivering.

I turn to Mara. 'I'm cold,' I say. 'And I'm still bleeding. Am I dying?'

'No,' she says. She holds my hand in her own clean, warm hand. 'No,' she says, again, a little too firmly.

We sit like that for a while and I start to feel sleepy as I rock the baby. 'How long?' Mara says, nudging me awake. 'How long have you been here?'

'I don't know,' I say.

'How early is she?'

'Three weeks,' I say.

'I can't get a phone signal,' she says. 'We need to get you seen to. How long since she was born?'

'I don't know,' I say again. 'A few minutes maybe.'

'And where the fuck is Pete?'

I shake my head. I try to explain, but not much comes out. 'Gone,' I try to say. I don't know if the word is audible.

'Alright, shhh,' says Mara. 'You need to stay nice and calm.' She puts the back of her hand against my forehead. I can see her looking at everything around me again: at the knife, and the vodka bottle, and my blood-stained feet. She concentrates for a few moments, taking it all in.

'We need to cut the cord,' she says. She's eyeing up the knife. She swallows hard. 'Alright,' she says, 'I've seen this done plenty of times. Been a birth partner twice before, so I guess this makes three. Can't be that hard, right?' She takes the cord between her fingers and, the way her fingers flinch, it must feel slippery. She works her way along the cord, until she's close to the baby. 'I think you need to put her down,' she says. I place the bundle on the ground, and again there's the tiny, scratchy sound, like a kitten coughing. The baby must be sick. Surely she should scream loudly, surely she would demand food and warmth more fiercely, if she were well?

Mara pinches the cord between her thumb and forefinger, just a few inches up from the baby's body. The towel has fallen away from her and the baby's tiny tummy is heaving up and down. All her little limbs are scrunched up. She looks primeval, like the re-animated fossil of an ancient bird. 'Love, you're going to have to help,' Mara says. 'This is a three-hander.' She braces the cord with her other hand, a few inches higher up. I reach for the knife, though every movement hurts, and when I hold it, the blade is shaking. 'Steady, girl,' Mara says, 'just go between my fingers. It won't take much pressure, just a bit of movement.' I line the knife up and I start to saw. The rope splices quickly and there are only a few drops of blood, black and thick, as it unravels. Mara is bundling the baby back into my arms.

'We need a band,' she says. 'You got any elastic bands round here?'

I shake my head. She looks around the place. 'Bloody hell,' she says and she takes a swig on the vodka bottle. 'Do I have to think of everything? Hair ties?' she says.

'Upstairs,' I say, 'bathroom cabinet.' She jumps up. She runs up the stairs and is back in a jiff with a little elastic tie. Everything about her – her calmness, her cleanness, her energy – seems impossible. But these things happen every day, they're happening again right now, only somewhere else. People are born, people are dying: it's all horribly possible. Mara just takes this in her stride. She unfolds the towel and finds the stump of cord, a little three-inch sprig extending from the baby's tummy. 'I don't know if this will work,' she says, 'but let's give it a try until we can get you seen to.' She ties the band around the end of the cord, looping it several times until it's tight. Then she folds the towel back around the baby: ever so careful, ever so tender.

'Listen,' she says. 'I don't want to scare you, but I came here to tell you and Pete something. They're evacuating us. Saying we have no choice now, that we have to leave. The wardens from the camp will be round in a couple of hours to try to evict us. We were going to stay firm, stage a sit-in with some blokes from our street. Anyway, the thing is, the thing I wanted to tell you is, they've evacuated the medical teams. Apparently they went a couple of days back. There's no one left in town to help you.'

She looks at me now, uncertainly. I don't know what to say. I can feel the baby squirming against my skin. I can feel her mouth opening and closing against my collar bone. I look down at her and see one of her eyes trembling. Her eyelid flinches a couple of times, and then, very slowly, as though she's being roused from the longest sleep, it begins to open –

'Listen,' she says. 'You need to come with us. I know what we'll do. And Paulie's going to agree, when I talk it through with him, when I explain the situation. We'll go to the camp. We'll take you there. There'll be doctors there, there's gotta be.'

– there are tiny lashes, which I hadn't seen before, and, as the eye slowly, drunkenly opens, there's an oily, dark iris, and a tiny pupil dilating wildly. She sees me. The baby sees me. The eye is spinning and swimming, and she looks right at me. And then, very slowly, her eye closes again.

'So I'm going to go and tell Paulie, and then we'll come back for you.'

'The camp?' I ask.

'Yeah,' she says. 'It's the only way we can get you treatment, I reckon.'

'If you take me there, they'll take your house,' I say. 'You might not be able to get it back.'

'Maybe,' she says.

'Why would you do that?' I say.

'I'm not going to leave you here on your own, am I, mate?' Mara says. 'And who knows: maybe they're right. Maybe the camps are safer.'

I don't reply. I watch the baby's face, waiting to see if her eye will flinch open again.

'Oh shit,' she says. 'You need to feed her. Try, try now. Her mouth's gaping.'

I stare at Mara. I hadn't even thought about feeding her. And thinking about it now – I can't. I can't just feed her. I don't know how to explain it to Mara, that I can't even try. Trying would feel too hopeful.

Mara looks at me for a long time and I shake my head. She swallows hard again, her soft throat jerking up and down.

'I could…' she says, and then looks down at the ground. 'I mean, she needs to feed and if you haven't got any formula… I guess you're probably worried about– '

I lift the child up to her. I push the baby into her arms. She looks at me and nods. And then she shrugs her top off her left shoulder, as if it's so easy, as if it's the easiest thing in the world. She pushes the baby's face up to her breast, and the baby's little beak works and works, not finding anything at first, or not latching right, but then, after a few moments, she's latched on, she's sucking the milk in tiny little gasps, and its running down her chin and down Mara's breast, and the baby's taking it. 'Right fierce latch, this little terrier's got,' Mara says. 'What a bite!'

I make a sound. It could be a laugh; it could be a death rattle. Mara links her fingers with mine while she feeds the baby, and then she says that everything is going to be ok.

'She won't need much,' Mara says. 'Her tummy's the size of a marble right now, that's what they told me when Iluka was born. But she'll need it often.' She hands the baby back to me.

'I'm not going to be gone long,' she says. 'We'll need to pack-up a few things. Then we'll come back in the car and I'll help you. There won't be much space, but,' she says, 'so it'll have to be essentials. One bag, right? That's what I'll tell Paulie. And we need to move fast. Listen, just don't worry. You stay here, don't you move. We'll come back, I'll sort things out, and we'll go together. I'm coming back for you, mate, and for this little one.'

And then she's gone, before I can say, Don't leave me. For Chrisake, don't leave me alone with the baby. I don't know how to love her. I don't know how to be that hopeful.

The baby's in my arms, so I cradle her again for a while, like Mara did. I think of Pete and I make myself look at her again. Her breath is fast and uneven, and her whole body palpitates on the turn of each little gasp. But she's doing it: this tiny thing is trying to live. The sky is beginning to turn to gold outside. The sun must be setting and I want to leave this scene behind: the blood-jelly and the knife and the empty bottle. It's hard to get up. I put the baby down and I manage it on the fourth attempt. I have to walk in a new way, moving real slow. I pick the baby up and I take her out to the edge of the porch. The sky over the mountains is a pink blaze. I think I can smell fire on the air. Perhaps it's my imagination? It's definitely your imagination, babe, Pete would say.

This is what won't happen: Pete won't put his arm around me and touch the baby's cheek with his fingertips. He won't tell me that he's going to take care of us. He won't look at the baby's tiny, curled fingers with so much fear for her that it makes his heart thump in his chest and in his throat, with so much fear that it makes him feel more alive and closer to death than he's ever been. And my mother will not hold the baby, or kiss her furrowed forehead, or tell her, when she's older and harder, pushing her dark hair out of her eyes, that even though it hurts her sometimes, she's proud of her fierceness. My mother will never sing hymns to us, or read to us, or name plants in her garden with us. And my mother will never hold me, and be pushed away, and still try to hold me again.

It's then that I hear the first one go: I hear a soft thud, like ripe fruit falling to the ground. My mother used to say that I was left under a mulberry bush, born as cleanly as a pear. But that was a lie. No one's born clean, I know that now. Everyone's born out of blood and fire. There's another little thud. And, a few moments later, another. This time I see something drop from the tree at the end of the garden. I hold the baby tight to my chest and I walk slowly to the edge of the border. I wait a moment, but there's no sound. I peer at the soil at the foot of the tree, and then I see it: a tiny little bird, a baby bird, fallen from a nest, and another baby bird just a few feet away from it. One of them is twitching on its side, its little legs scrabbling at nothing. The other is perfectly still. And I know before I look at them closely what it is that I will see; that their eyes will be fused, the grey skin sealing them into darkness. I stare out across the valley, where no lights glimmer now, and I see the full panorama: the pink sky above the mountains is hazing into purple as smoke rises in the distance. Behind the mountains everything is burning. The world is on fire behind the mountains. And I know that the forest won't protect us. The forest doesn't want us here, filthying up the air and the water and the soil. The forest knows what we've done to this land: it's watched us steal it and mine it and run poison into its seams. The forest wants rid of us.

Behind me, another thud, heavier this time: an adult bird, blurred into blackness, hitting the side of the house and fitting on the ground. Another bird falls from the tree in front of me. And then it begins in earnest: the mewling and distant screeching and cawing, as the animals, concealed all around me, begin to be sealed in to their hiding places – suffocated in the undergrowth, deep in the earth, in their burrows in the roots of the trees – as they start to spin and scream and claw in blind, hopeless fear of their own skin.

I turn away from the mountains. Mara's at the gate. She's standing very still, listening to the animal noises rising all around us. The sky above her is deep and lustrous as melted bronze, a sky-mirror full of fire. Mara puts her hands up to her ears, digs her fingers into her scalp. And then she shakes her head hard and she's through the gate, running towards me. 'Alice! We've got to go,' she shouts, and catches my arm hard, 'Iluka and Paulie are in the car and we're going, right now, right now, all of us are going.'

I gather the baby hard into my chest, and the fire on the air is on my tongue and in my belly now too. I am part of this; me and Mara and Iluka and Paulie, and my mother, and Pete too – Pete too – and all of our dead who we carry with us, and the baby, this baby in my arms who only wants to live, we're all under this burning sky together and we can't stay safe, there is no safe. The baby moves her face against my chest, opening her little red mouth up to the world and asking it to feed her. I'm beginning to feel warm and alive again. I'll go with Mara. We'll go together, and I'll take care of her, I'll take care of this tiny creature curled in my chest. I will not let us be sealed in. I've fought through my own skin and I'll carry on fighting, tooth and bloody claw, until I find a way to have hope. Until I find a way to love her.

'C'mon,' says Mara. 'You'll have to leave everything. We're going now.'

And as we move together, me and the baby and Mara, the world is new to me again, a great burning ball of fire and pain and hope.

ABOUT THE AUTHOR

Naomi Booth is a fiction writer and academic. Her novella, *The Lost Art of Sinking*, emerged from research into the literary history of swooning, and won the Saboteur Award for Best Novella 2016 as well as being selected for New Writing North's Read Regional campaign 2017. Her first novel, *Sealed*, is a gripping modern fable on motherhood. She is currently working on a new novel and collection of short stories, and an academic monograph on passing out.

In 2018 Naomi was named in the *Guardian*'s 'Fresh Voices: 50 Writers to Read Now'. She was also picked for the 'Not the Booker' shortlist and was long-listed for the *Sunday Times* EFG Short Story Award.

Naomi grew up in West Yorkshire, UK, and now lives in York. She lectures in Creative Writing and Literature.

ACKNOWLEDGEMENTS

Enormous thanks go to Nathan Connolly and Amelia Collingwood at Dead Ink Books, Lucia Walker, Emma Bailey and Sabhbh Curran at Curtis Brown, and Gary Budden and Davi Lancett at Titan Books, for their enthusiasm and work on this book. Thank you, also, to all of the readers who first supported this project through Dead Ink and made this book a reality.

Michael Fake—who initially told me this story was too horrible to write, thereby inspiring me to continue it—also provided support of a more conventional and indispensable nature: thank you. I am grateful to early readers who had to pick through some chaotic gore, in particular: James Booth, Abi Curtis, Oliver Morgan, Sameer Rahim and Toby Smart. Special thanks for brilliant writing advice and encouragement go to Tom Bunstead, Camilla Bostock, Kieran Devaney, Dulcie Few, Laura Joyce, Helen Jukes and Tom Houlton. For their long-standing support, I am grateful to Tom Chivers, Nasser Hussain, Kate Murray-Browne, Sophie Nicholls, Nicholas Royle and JT Welsch. I am also thankful for continuing conversations with my colleagues and students at York St John University.

Thank you to my parents, Jane and Ian Booth, who helped me to find time to finish off the writing after the birth of my daughter and who continue to support me even when my work is too disgusting for them to read. I am lucky to count many generous and talented women as friends, and they inspire everything I do: thank you Kechi Ajuonuma, Janine Bradbury, Clare Brook, Lena Graff, Rebecca Hawkins, Sophie Hamza, Tricia Mundy, Katy O'Neill, Emma Phillips, Lucy Rice, Poppy Templeton and Ruby Templeton. To the fiercest and most tenacious girl I know, Betty Fake, thank you for teaching me about the importance of hopefulness.

THE BEAUTY
Aliya Whiteley

Somewhere away from the cities and towns, a group of men and boys gather around the fire each night to listen to their stories in the Valley of the Rocks. Theirs is a world without women, and the men are waiting to pass into the night. Meet Nate, the storyteller, and the new secrets he brings back from the woods. Where the women's bodies were buried, something strange is growing…

Discover the Beauty.

'Aliya Whiteley's fierce, hallucinatory *The Beauty* is the brilliant gender-bending, post-apocalyptic horror fable the world needs right now. This book messed me up, in the best way possible.'
Paul Tremblay, author of *A Head Full of Ghosts*

"What a refreshing gust of tiny spores this novella explodes into, and I inhaled them all with glee."
Adam Nevill, author of *The Ritual*

THE CABIN AT THE END OF THE WORLD
Paul Tremblay

Seven-year-old Wen and her parents, Eric and Andrew, are vacationing at a remote cabin on a quiet New Hampshire lake, with their closest neighbours more than two miles in either direction. As Wen catches grasshoppers in the front yard, a stranger unexpectedly appears in the driveway. Leonard is the largest man Wen has ever seen but he is young and friendly. Leonard and Wen talk and play until Leonard abruptly apologises and tells Wen, "None of what's going to happen is your fault."

So begins an unbearably tense, gripping tale of paranoia, sacrifice, apocalypse, and survival that escalates to a shattering conclusion, one in which the fate of a loving family and quite possibly all of humanity are intertwined.

"A tremendous book – thought-provoking and terrifying, with tension that winds up like a chain…Tremblay's personal best. It's that good."
Stephen King

THE RIFT
Nina Allan

**WINNER OF THE 2017 BSFA AWARD FOR BEST NOVEL
WINNER OF THE KITSCHIES RED TENTACLE 2017**

Selena and Julie are sisters. As children they were close, but as they grow older, a rift develops between them. There are greater rifts, however. Julie goes missing aged seventeen. It will be twenty years before Selena sees her again. When Julie reappears, she tells Selena an incredible story about how she has spent time on another planet. Does Selena dismiss her sister as the victim of delusions, or believe her, and risk her own sanity?

"One of the best books published this year in any genre."
Strange Horizons

**"Her literary sensibility fuses the fantastic
and the mundane to great effect."**
Guardian

**"Moving, subtle, and ambiguous, this is
a good pick for literary-SF fans."**
Booklist

TITANBOOKS.COM

For more fantastic fiction, author events, exclusive
excerpts, competitions, limited editions and more

VISIT OUR WEBSITE
titanbooks.com

LIKE US ON FACEBOOK
facebook.com/titanbooks

FOLLOW US ON TWITTER
@TitanBooks

EMAIL US
readerfeedback@titanemail.com